ABORIGINAL LEGENDS

ANIMAL TALES

A. W. REED

Reed New Holland

Published in Australia by
Reed New Holland
an imprint of New Holland Publishers (Australia) Pty Ltd
Sydney • Auckland • London • Cape Town
14 Aquatic Drive Frenchs Forest NSW 2086 Australia
218 Lake Road Northcote Auckland New Zealand
86 Edgware Road London W2 2EA United Kingdom
80 McKenzie Street Cape Town 8001 South Africa

First published in 1978 by Reed Books Pty Ltd
Reprinted in 1982, 1984, 1987, 1988, 1989, 1991, 1992, 1993, 1994, 1997
Reprinted in 1998, 1999, 2002 and 2005 by Reed New Holland

Designer: Luisa Laino
Cover illustration: Kim Roberts
Typesetter: Midland Typesetters
Printer: Australian Print Group

10 9 8 7 6 5

National Library of Australia Cataloguing-in-Publication Data:

Aboriginal Legends
ISBN 1 87633 415 0

(1) Aborigines, Australian – Legends. 1. Reed.
Alexander Wyclif, 1980–1979.

398.20994

CONTENTS

INTRODUCTION

This book provides a small selection of Aboriginal legends dealing with animals and men, from the vast range of such stories. It is hoped that a variety of legends, many of them about the origin of different forms of animal life, coming from tribes scattered across the continent, will show the fertile imagination of the Aboriginal, and his closeness to nature. Closeness is perhaps an inadequate term. Rather we could say that there was a 'oneness' in men and all other aspects of nature. Both men and animals were part of an endless Dreamtime that began with the deeds of totemic ancestors. Their deeds are part of life, and men are part of animals, as animals are of men, therefore both are usually capitalised in the text. This is not the place to discuss the complex subject of totemism, but it is necessary to refer to it to understand that in these Dreamtime tales, men and animals may change from one to thc other, or share the form and nature of both. It is difficult for we who are within Western culture to understand a concept that is inherent in Aboriginal man. The clue to understanding lies in the Dreamtime. In that Dream world, man dreamed splendid dreams of kinship with everything that surrounded him and invented glorious tales, as well as horrific ones, to provide a satisfying account of the origin of natural life with which he was so familiar, investing what most of us accept as commonplace with the supernatural.

There is poetry in these stories—poetry that is difficult to capture in another language. It is a problem I have faced for half a lifetime in retelling legends, not only of Aboriginals, but of Polynesians and those of other races and cultures. A literal account would frequently provide a text which would have little impact on a reader of European ancestry or listener—though it must be admitted that the legends of the Aranda tribe have been lovingly converted to English by Professor T. G. H. Strehlow, preserving the beauty of words and forms of speech of those who live close to nature in the ever-present Dreamtime.

In striking contrast to this treatment, Roland Robinson, a poet of distinction, has taken legends related to him by learned, semi-literate Aboriginals and presented them exactly as spoken. These were men who preserved the lore of their fathers in the soul-destroying environment of European contact, retaining something of the pristine freshness of the dawn of man in a totally different environment to those of the Central and Northern tribes.

The method I have adopted is rather different. I have had neither opportunity nor ability to collect the legends of the original Australians at first-hand; but I have profited from the personal contacts and research of dedicated field-workers and have retold the legends they have gathered, as they appeal to me, with as little distortion as possible. Admittedly they are a product of the 1970s, written by one whose skin is a different colour, and whose environment is completely foreign to that of the Aboriginals who devised them. If by chance they give enjoyment to others and some small insight into the treasury of Aboriginal lore, something will have been gained.

But can the essential spirit of these tales of antiquity be conveyed to others by a Western storyteller of the twentieth century? It is doubtful, for modern phraseology is not suited to the relation of events of what is a world apart from life today, and a Biblical style of narration, resorted to by some writers, even less so. Further, is one justified in attempting to introduce modern storytelling devices into a legend that has been transmitted through generations of Aboriginal tellers of tales, using the media of song and dance as well as the spoken word, or to embroider a narrative that makes no pretence of a plot, but is rather a re-living of the experiences of a daytime or a lifetime? These are questions for which the reader must find an answer, and provide his own judgment.

The legends of the first Australians are not confined to animals. Exciting adventures and experiences will be found in other collections, some being included in *Myths and Legends of Australia* and *Aboriginal Fables* by the writer, as well as in collections made by those who gathered material at first-hand. A distinction, hazy at times, should also be made between folk-lore, with which the present collection is concerned, and myths relating to the Great Father Spirit, the Creator (who is known by several names) and the totemic ancestors and their journeys and deeds. These are the subject of a companion volume, *Aboriginal Myths*.

CHAPTER ONE
REPTILE PEOPLE

Before examining a few typical legends of reptiles and kindred species, it is well to recall the widespread belief in the existence of the Rainbow Snake, symbolic of rain, water, and the products of rain, all vitally important to tribes that occupied or ventured into the vast desert regions of the interior. Many tribes believed that, were it not for the Rainbow Snake, life would cease to exist.

The extent to which the Rainbow Snake entered into fertility rites is indicated by the frequency of his (or her) appearance in sacred designs and drawings. Water was the life-giving element. The Snake that brought rain was the life-giving force in religious rites. Medicine-men whom he killed and brought to life were able to conjure up rain clouds by appealing to him and performing the necessary rites.

One of the great totemic ancestors was preceded on her journey by the Rainbow Snake which cleared the way by uprooting trees and causing rivers to flow to the sea. He symbolised the storms and floods that caused the rivers to rise. In Arnhem Land he protected sacred lore by sending floods to drown those who offended against it. In this area, so rich in art forms, he was called Julunggul or Yurlunggui. In the Kimberleys he was associated with childbirth.

The Aboriginal attitude towards snakes is therefore vastly different to that of most white people. The close association of the Rainbow snakes with totemic ancestors and their beneficent role in providing water is an indication that reptiles were not in any way regarded with revulsion. The fact that they made a welcome contribution to the meagre larder in the drier regions of the continent was of considerable importance to Aboriginals. Europeans who are accustomed to handling snakes, though treating them with respect, have a mental attitude towards them probably akin to that of the Aboriginals themselves, who regard them as objectively and impassively as the other forms of life that contribute to their welfare.

The Snake People of Ayers Rock

The importance of snakes in Aboriginal mythology is illustrated by identification of many of the features on the southern face of Ayers Rock with the Kunia (carpet-snakes) and the Liru (poisonous snakes), and the battles they fought. Other features of the Rock are identified with various species of lizards as well as animals.

The two kinds of Snake people, poisonous and non-poisonous, lived together at a waterhole called Pugabuga. The more restive members of the Kunia tribe became dissatisfied with their surroundings and decided to migrate to a flat sandhill where there was a limitless supply of water. At the end of the Dreamtime the sandhill was changed to the rock known to Australians as Ayers Rock, but as Uluru to the Pitjandjara tribe.

When the sandhill was transformed into a rock, the Kunia people were also changed to stone and can be seen as boulders or features of the Rock. Coolamons, wooden dishes for carrying water, grass-seed and other commodities, knives, spears, and grinding stones were also changed. The caves where men, women, and children took refuge could be descried in the irregularities of the rock face by the imaginative tribespeople of a later age. The beards of the old men, the tracks men made to fetch water from the Uluru waterhole, all can be traced on the face of Ayers Rock.

The Liru people, the venomous Snake men, struck off in a different direction, going towards Mount Olga and preying on the peace-loving people they met.

One of the Kunia women gave birth to a baby in a cave in the Rock—a cave that was later resorted to by Aboriginal women in labour in the belief that the spirit of that Carpet-snake woman would ensure an easy and painless delivery.

No sooner had the baby of the Kunia clan been born than Bulari, for that was her name, saw a party of Liru warriors coming towards her. She called to the Carpet-snake men to come to her aid, first spitting disease and death at the warriors before taking refuge in a nearby gorge. Working themselves into a fury with shouts and war songs, the Liru men attacked the Kunias. Many on both sides were killed in the battle.

The signs of the conflict can be clearly traced on the Rock. The bodies of the dead men are there, and the open mouths of the warriors who shouted defiance at their enemies. A long fissure and a shorter one can be seen in the rock face. The cracks in the rock represent places where a young Kunia warrior slashed open the leg of the leader of the raiding party. The longer cut was made when the knife was sharp, the shorter one as the tip of the knife broke off.

The Kunia warrior's triumph was short-lived. The Liru leader wounded him so severely that he was forced to crawl away on hands and knees, and bled to death at the side of a watercourse. The Pitjandjara believed that by shouting a certain word his spirit could still send water cascading from the hole in the rock where he died.

When the mother of the young warrior heard of her son's death, she seized her digging stick, which was impregnated with the same spirit of death used by the mother in the cave, and descended on the Liru leader like an avenging fury. So deep was her grief and fierce her desire for revenge, that the man had no time to defend himself. Bringing the stick down with all the force she could muster, she cracked his skull, severing his nose from his face. A split rock, more than twenty metres in length standing apart from the cliff, represents the nose of the warrior, four holes in the cliff his eyes and nasal passages, and the water stains on the face of the cliff his blood.

A striking mouth-shaped cave is the open mouth of the grief-stricken mother. She fled with the survivors to the eastern end of the Rock of Kuniapiti, where she met the remaining refugees. The Liru men had made simultaneous attacks on various groups of Carpet-snake people and only a few women and children were left alive. The mother who had avenged the death of her son by killing the Liru leader, and her brother, were so distressed that they 'sang' the spirits of death into themselves and died at Kuniapiti, where they had taken refuge.

Many boulders and peculiar depressions, protuberances, cracks, and stains on the Rock commemorate the massacre of the harmless Carpet-snake people, whose bodies are boulders, their hair the tufts of bushes that have taken root in the rock face.* The stones that are the bodies of the mother and brother of the young warrior were used in increase ceremonies in the belief that rubbing them would increase the Carpet-snake population and thus provide more food.

After the raid on Uluru, the Liru men linked up with a tribe of men of gigantic stature, the Pungalunga. The combined force then attempted to wipe out the mythical Kunduna Snakes in the Tomkinson Range. In attempting this foolish enterprise the Liru people were completely exterminated.

Snakes and Turtles

In view of the preceding tale of the conflict between poisonous and non-poisonous snakes, it is interesting to learn how some species became venomous.

The fact of the matter, said the wise men of one tribe, is that at one time all Snakes were harmless while Turtles possessed forked tongues and carried the poison glands.

In those days there was great competition between Men, Turtles, and Snakes for eels which were highly esteemed as food. No one was satisfied, each of the three clans claiming that the others were taking more than their fair share. The eels were even less satisfied!

Turtles had another cause for complaint. The females of the Turtle tribe were accustomed to laying their eggs among the reeds at the edge of lakes,

* In his book *Ayers Rock* (Angus and Robertson), from which the information in this section has been gleaned, Charles P. Mountford includes a magnificent collection of photographs of the natural features of the Rock and explains their significance.

pools, and streams; but unfortunately for the Turtles, Snakes and Human Beings were even more partial to Turtle eggs than to eels. And since the Snake tribe was not poisonous, its people were harried by hunters who relished a tasty feed of Snake meat.

And, curiously enough, Men and Women were not very happy either, because they were afraid of the Turtles—and with good cause. When they stooped down to gather eggs from the nests at the base of the reeds, Turtles would swim rapidly through the water and, before the egg-gatherers could draw back, would leap up and bite them on the tongue. A distressing business for the Men and Women who were gathering food, for the poisoned teeth of Turtles inflicted a fatal wound. It was useless to try to defend themselves, for the carapace of a Turtle deflected the heaviest blows of spear and club.

Everyone was dissatisfied. The Humans were the first to initiate action to improve their lot. They sent a deputation to Spur-wing Plover, who was noted for his ingenuity, to seek his help. Plover was also an eel hunter, and a very effective one, more so than the Snakes or Human Beings. Before he went on an eeling expedition he smeared white clay on his armpits as a kind of camouflage. Equipping himself with two spears, one in each hand, he would take up a position on the bank of a stream or pond and stand motionless, waiting for an eel to come close to the edge. With a lightning stroke of one of his spears he would impale it and throw it on the bank. This was how the Human hunters caught the eels. The secret of Plover's success, which Men had never succeeded in imitating, was his skill in handling two spears, enabling him to strike with either hand, no matter where the eel appeared.

In spite of this, Men fished for eels so persistently that the supply was becoming depleted. Plover feared the day might come when it might be difficult to find enough to satisfy his appetite.

When the Men came to him asking for help in their feud with the Turtles, Plover was delighted. He could see a way of reducing the Human population while rendering the Turtles harmless.

His first move was to call the Snakes together. When they were assembled he suggested that it would be a good idea if they changed heads with the Turtles.

'Why should we do that?' they asked. 'What good would it do for us?'

'I'm surprised you ask that question,' Plover replied. 'Just think. If you possess their poison sacs, you'll be able to defend yourselves against the Humans. Oh, I know that they'll keep on doing their best to kill you, but it will be so much more difficult that many of you will be able to save your lives. And in addition, remember that you, too, will be able to kill many of them, just as the Turtles do now. More so, because you live on the land, whereas the Turtles have to wait until they go to the water's edge before they can get close enough to bite their tongues.'

It was a convincing argument. Provided Plover could get the Turtles to agree, the Snakes were in favour of exchanging heads.

Plover next went to see the Turtles. He explained his plan, stipulating that if they accepted it, they must agree to a small request of his own.

'If we give our heads to the Snakes, we'll be defenceless against the Humans,' the Turtles argued. 'We'll lose all our eggs, and in another generation there'll be no more Turtles!'

'Not so,' said Plover. 'In the first place, the Snakes live on land and will have many more opportunities of biting Humans than you ever have. That should reduce their numbers considerably.'

'It's a point,' one of the old-man Turtles said reflectively, 'but I'm still not convinced. Even though there may be fewer Humans, our eggs will be even more vulnerable. That means that fewer Humans will be able to gather more eggs with impunity.'

'That is so,' Plover admitted. 'But I can show you how to cure that problem. I've often thought you are foolish leaving your eggs among the reeds where anyone can pick them up. Why don't you bury them? If you cover them with sand or soil, no one will find them; and the sun will warm them. They'll hatch more quickly that way.'

'But the young Turtles won't know how to get into the water,' the old-man Turtle objected.

'Oh yes, they will. If they don't know the way themselves, the rains will come and wash them into the stream.'

The Turtles debated for a long time while Plover waited to hear the decision. When it was made it was favourable. They agreed to his plan.

'Now for my request,' Plover reminded them.

They looked at him warily.

'A very simple request,' he assured them. 'Leave the big eels for me. You can take as many little ones as you can catch.'

The Turtles agreed it was a fair price to pay for the new kind of life they would lead. All that remained was to organise a place and time for the exchange of heads. When it was all over, Turtles found a safer place for their eggs; but without their poison sacs they were helpless to defend themselves. Human Beings found it harder to find Turtle eggs and were in constant danger from Snakes. The eggs were equally difficult for Snakes to find, and they were hunted ruthlessly by Humans. Spur-wing Plover was the only one who gained any advantage from the transaction and even that was doubtful, for as the supply of small eels diminished, there were few of them to grow into large eels.

It is probable that no one, Turtle, Snake, Plover, or Human, was any happier than before.

In another part of Australia, the poison sac was supposed to be a possession of Goannas which was stolen from them by the Black Snake. The only consolation Goannas had was the discovery of a certain plant that counteracted the effects of their own poison when they were bitten by Black Snakes.

Death to the Giant Snake

In this romantic folk tale the principal characters are Men and Women, and the villian of the piece is a real-life snake instead of a Snake-man. It concerns a young man and woman who were greatly in love with each other.

Their future life together seemed assured, for they had been promised to each other in marriage. The man had completed his initiation tests, enduring the ordeals with proper stoicism. As soon as he returned from the hunting expedition, the spoils of which were to be given to the parents of his promised bride, she would be given to him.

While he was absent, the girl went into the bush to collect honey to add to the coming feast. It proved difficult to find and she wandered a long way from the camp. Her search took her into a stony valley, far from her usual haunts. An unusual silence brooded over it. Not a single bird was in the valley, and she missed the usual rustle and chirping of insects. She was about to retrace her steps when her eyes lighted on a cluster of eggs lying in the shade of a large boulder. They were the largest eggs she had ever seen. These, she thought, would make a splendid addition to the coming feast, better than honey, which could be gathered at any time.

She bent to pick them up and place them in her dilly-bag, when she heard the sound of something slithering over the rocks. Before she had time to move or even to open her mouth to scream, the coils of an enormous brown and yellow snake encircled her waist. Another loop fell over her shoulders. They tightened round her body, squeezing the life out of her, crushing her bones to pulp. As quietly as it had come, the snake glided away, its colours merging into the arid background of jumbled rocks. It had come and gone without malice, but determined to protect its precious cluster of eggs.

Two days went by before her relatives discovered her mangled body. Seeing the snake eggs lying on the ground close to her outstretched hand, they realised what had happened to her.

'So young, and so foolish to attempt to steal the eggs of the giant snake,' her mother said tearfully, as they laid the broken body at her feet. 'When her promised husband returns, how can we tell him of her fate?'

The camp fires were beginning to gleam in the dusk as he returned. In spite of his long trek and the heavy burden on his back, his step was light, his eyes shining at the thought of the new life that would begin that night.

On his back was a load, big or bigger than any one man had ever brought into the camp—a kangaroo, a wombat, and the thighs of an emu.

'This is my gift to you,' he said to the mother and father who sat in silence before him.

Their reply was as devastating as it was unexpected:

'You have come in time for her burial, son who was to be.'

The young man could scarcely contain his grief as the story of her death was unfolded. As a blooded warrior, he held back his tears and said coldly, 'Why have you not buried her?'

'Her body has just been found this very day,' her father said.

'Then I shall follow her and claim her spirit. The wirinun will mend her broken bones, and I shall restore her spirit and breathe life into her.'

'That you may not do,' her father said sternly. 'Her spirit is now in the realm to which all women must go, and the one who killed her is still alive. Where does your duty lie?'

The young man looked steadily at him. He had no more words. He turned and went to the house of the unmarried men. No one dared speak to him. His grief was his to bear alone.

As the days passed there was whispering in the village. Everyone had expected that he would set out in search of the snake that had killed his promised wife, but he sought no information from those who had found the girl's body. He took no part in the dances and songs at night. He said little to anyone, nor did he seem to hear what they said to him. He took part in the hunt each day, but at night he was wrapped in a cloak of silence. The old women shook their heads.

'He will die,' one said. 'He wishes to join the girl in the spirit world.'

'He will never succeed,' said another. 'There is one such world for men, and another for women.'

'You are wrong,' said a third. 'He is silent because he is lost in thought. Do you, who have never seen one of these snakes, think a man can go out with his spear and put such a snake to death? When I was young, I saw one. I shall never forget that day. Look at these grey hairs. They are not grey with age. They turned from black to grey and then to white on the day I saw that monstrous brown and yellow horror.'

'What was it like? Tell us about it,' said another.

'You've heard me tell it often enough,' she cackled. 'Telling is not enough. If you had seen it, you would know what I mean.'

'Then what do you think the young fellow will do?' asked the woman who had wanted the story retold. She dropped her voice to a whisper. 'Do you think he is afraid?'

'No. He has no fear, that one. We must have patience.'

But little patience was needed. The following morning the young warrior surprised everyone by saying, 'Who will come with me to gather beefwood gum?'

He sounded so cheerful that everyone looked at him in surprise.

'Why do you want gum? We have plenty. You can have some of ours if you need it.'

'It's fresh gum I want.'

He laughed at them, looking more like his old self. 'If you help me gather it I'll show you what I'm going to do with it.'

Overcome with curiosity, they followed him without further question. After the gum had been gathered, he made no attempt to return to the camp but led them to the valley of the giant snakes. Taking one of his closest friends with him, he left the others at the mouth of the valley, warning them not to venture any further. Making as little noise as possible, the two young men gathered armfuls of fallen branches and built a platform in an overhanging tree.

'Now you can make as much noise as you like,' the young man said to his friend. They shouted at the top of their voices, joined by the others who were waiting at the mouth of the valley.

'Again!' he called as the clamour died away, and again the valley threw the sound back and forth between the cliffs.

Suddenly—there it was, the gigantic brown and yellow snake, its head swaying from side to side as if searching for the source of the noise. It was followed by a swarm of smaller snakes with the same colouring. It was evident that the eggs the girl had intended to take home, for the gathering of which she had died, had hatched into a monstrous brood.

The moment of vengeance had arrived, but for the watchers the manner of its coming was still a mystery.

Their curiosity was at last rewarded. The two men in the trees took lumps of newly gathered gum from their dilly-bags and kneaded them into large balls. The mother snake had located them on their platform and was uncoiling her vast body, her tongue quivering between widely-opened jaws, her head coming close to the platform. When a ball of gum fell into her open mouth her jaws closed like a spring trap, her teeth sinking deeply into the gum.

The young men pelted the baby snakes with the gum and succeeded in sealing their gaping jaws as those of their mother had been sealed.

There was no pity in the hearts of any of the men who came to the valley that day. Bubbur, the biggest of snakes, had killed the loveliest daughter of their clan. Her children were small only by comparison, each as thick through the body as a man's leg, each growing in size and strength to some day match its mother's enormous bulk.

With sealed jaws the small snakes were no longer dangerous. The onlookers rushed into the valley and attacked the brood, mother and offspring, until all were dead.

'The Bubburs have been scarce in the land since then,' wrote that great teller of Aboriginal folk-tales, Mrs Langloh Parker, 'though their name carries terror yet to its hearer. Their size has grown with time, and fear has stretched their measurements, until even the strongest and wariest feel a tremor when the name of the brown and yellow Bubbur is mentioned.'

Goanna makes a Canoe

From the far north of Queensland comes the story of how Goanna made the first bark canoe. It seems probable that Goanna's habit of climbing trees and clinging to the bark is responsible for the story of canoe-making as told by the observant Aboriginals of that area.

The Goanna man had been experimenting in the construction of a canoe. As no such vessel had ever been dreamed of, his efforts were clumsy. When the canoe was completed he launched it, jumped in and pushed it out into the sheltered bay, where he began to fish. In a short time the water that seeped through the roughly sewn seams was up to his knees. Thoroughly disgusted, he swam ashore and watched the disintegrating sheet of bark being carried away by the tide.

He sat lost in thought, going over in his mind what he had done, determined to find what he had done wrong. For a long time he brooded, but at last the frown left his brow. He knew how to rectify his mistakes. It was no use trying to patch up the old canoe, even if he could reach it. It was floating, almost submerged, far out in the bay. He walked upstream until he came to a suitable tree, and lit a fire at a little distance.

The method of construction he had devised has been admirably described by Ursula McConnel in her account of the Munkan legend 'The Making of a Bark Canoe by the Goanna'.*

'He climbs a tree; cuts a sheet of messmate bark; lays it over the fire; scorches it; pulls it out and lays it down near the river. He cuts fine bamboo; burns the point in the fire; splits the stalk down, flattens it, softens it down with his knife.

'He folds the sheet of bark down the middle and sews up one end; sews, sews, sews, pushing the point of the cane through the holes made with the pointed wallaby-bone stiletto. Then he sews up the other end; both ends he sews up, pushing the cane through. Then he cuts off the ends slantwise, inwards and downwards. Then he breaks short sticks; puts a stick on each side, laying them crosswise to keep the canoe stretched outwards. The bark he fastens by running string across to each side of the canoe and tightening it.

---

* Ursula McConnel, *Myths of the Munkan* (Melbourne University Press). The author is grateful for permission to include this extract.

'The splayed foot of a mangrove stem he cuts for a paddle; planes it down; heats it in the fire; bends it to straighten it.'

Now, well equipped with canoe and paddle, Goanna launched the canoe in the river, stepped into it confidently, and paddled downstream. As he went he leant over the side. The canoe did not capsize. He kept looking until he saw a fish. He raised his spear and impaled a very surprised fish on the three-pronged head. He speared another fish and another. By the time he reached the bay, many speared fish were lying at his feet in the canoe. The Goanna man felt pleased with himself.

The habit of tree-climbing remains with him, ever since the day he climbed a messmate tree to strip it of its bark. And it is up tree trunks that he still scuttles, when alarmed by intruders.

Goannas and Porcupines

The tree-climbing ability of Goannas is an important factor in a legend related by the tribes of the Murrumbidgee district. Goannas had come to this region shortly after all the animals had left the thousand islands of the northern seas and arrived in Australia in the canoe belonging to Whale (see page 53). Goannas were among these pioneers. They were an industrious people, noted for their patience and skill in growing food in the land from which they came, and living on the products of the soil.

Unhappily, their nature changed when they were settled in the southern part of the continent. They grew lazy, deceitful, and envious of others. They did not hesitate to steal provisions and, losing their appetite for vegetable food, developed a liking for meat. Flesh of any kind was welcome—small lizards, four-footed animals, so long as they were small and defenceless, and the flesh of larger animals, provided someone else had taken the trouble to kill them.

The most peculiar part of it all was that other animals seemed quite unaware of the changed habits of the Goannas. They had no suspicion that they were the thieves who stole their choicest pieces of meat. This applied even to the wives of the Goannas who, of course, belonged to other moieties. When their husbands reluctantly shared food with them they had no idea that, as often as not, it has been stolen, often from those of their own tribe.

One day the Goannas heard that the Porcupines had arranged to round up all the game in their vicinity. They proposed to spread out in a large circle, gradually closing in, driving the animals before them until they were penned into a small enclosure where they could be killed at leisure.

The head man of the Goanna tribe went to the leader of the hunt and offered the services of his own men.

'No thank you,' said the Porcupine leader. 'We don't need any help. Your offer surprises me. I thought you were all vegetarians. What do you know about game animals?'

'Nothing. Nothing at all,' the Goanna replied hastily. 'I didn't mean to suggest that we would take an active part in your expedition. I meant we could help in other ways.'

The head man of the Porcupines made no reply, but the inquiring look on his face was as good as a question.

Goanna racked his brain.

'Honey!' he said with sudden inspiration. 'That's it. Honey. Your men will be busy chasing the animals or whatever it is you do. Far too busy to look for honey, which would be a good thing to sweeten the meal tonight, wouldn't it? My men are skilled honey thieves—I mean honey seekers. Much better than yours, I suspect,' he went on glibly, gaining confidence. 'Porcupines are not well adapted for tree-climbing, no matter how good they may be as hunters. Let my men come behind you as you close in. I guarantee you'll have a pleasant surprise at the end of the day.'

After exacting a promise that there would be no interference in the hunt, Porcupine agreed to let the Goannas take part.

There was no doubt of the Goannas' skill in locating the nests of the bees. One of them caught a bee and tied a scrap of down to it. When the insect was released the Goannas were able to follow it to its nest high in a tree trunk. When they came to the branch where the honey was hidden in a hollow, they chopped at the trunk with their axes, leading the Porcupines to think they were chopping steps to help them climb the tree.

The hunt proved successful, a large number of possums being killed. Several coolamons of honey were equally welcome, for the Porcupines had a sweet tooth.

The Goannas ceremoniously carried the coolamons to the Porcupines, inviting them to take as much as they wanted. In other ways, too, they were painfully solicitous of the welfare of the Porcupines.

'You must be tired after that long chase,' their leader said. 'We can see what splendid hunters you are. We are weak creatures compared with you. We hope you will feel refreshed after eating this delicious honey. Why don't you all lie down and have a sleep? While you're resting we'll light the fires and roast the meat for you. When you wake up it will be waiting for you.'

The Porcupines lay down and watched the preparations drowsily. As the fires burned up and the smell of roasting meat filled the air, the Porcupines could not keep their eyes open. One after the other they dropped off to sleep.

Darkness fell, the stars came out, the moon rose over the distant hills and looked down on a peaceful scene. A glade in the bush, surrounded by tall trees. Porcupines sleeping peacefully. Goannas going about on tiptoe to avoid waking the sleepers, busily feeding the fires and occasionally turning the roasting possums.

High up in one of the tallest trees a solitary Goanna was keeping an eye on the sleepers, ready to give the alarm if one of them should waken.

Presently he gave a long-drawn screech. One of the Porcupines was sitting up, yawning and scratching himself, looking with some interest at the activities of the Goannas. As the air was rent by the alarm the scene changed from peace to frenzied activity. The Porcupine sprang to his feet, while others stretched themselves and sat up in alarm.

The Goannas were ready. They had taken the precaution of laying the possums in the ovens with their tails protruding outwards. Each Goanna seized two of the possums by their tails and scampered off with them to the trees. The last to go was the head man. He was burdened with four possums, two in each hand, and followed more slowly.

By this time it dawned on the Porcupines that the Goannas were robbing them of their meal. They raced after them. It was almost too late. All but the over-burdened leader were safely up the tree. He was in a sorry plight, cornered by the Porcupines just as the possums had been caught earlier in the day. He dodged backwards and forwards, trying to reach the tree, but in vain. Every step he took was blocked by a Porcupine, whose leader came up with a brand snatched from the fire. He beat the Goanna with it mercilessly, leaving burnt patches down his back. Finally he wrested the possums from the thief and let him go. The poor fellow crawled slowly up the trunk of the tree, more dead than alive, and fell into the arms of his men. They were not over-sympathetic. After all, they had most of the possums, cooked to a turn, and were able to enjoy a satisfying meal, while the Porcupines, far below, had to content themselves with a small serving of the four remaining animals.

It was many months before the head man of the Goannas recovered from the burns and welts on his back. He was scarred for life, and his descendants bear the same marks. Worse still, the secret vices of the Goanna tribe had been revealed to the world; never again would the Porcupines allow them to take part in a hunting expedition.

The Lizard who Came from Nowhere

It would seem that in folklore lizards are coupled with goannas as thieves. It may be that their habit of darting into hiding when alarmed had led men to think that they are guilty of thievish practices.

Long before these reptiles became common, a small boy suddenly appeared in an isolated village. No one knew where he came from. The people who lived at the camp were so far from any other clan or tribe that it was impossible for him to have come from a neighbouring encampment. Had he been lost when straying from a family on walkabout? That was the likeliest solution. But the fact that he could speak their own language perfectly seemed to make the supposition far-fetched.

He was questioned closely by the elders, and then by women who tried to gain his friendship, without result. He was prepared to talk about anything under the sun or moon except where he came from. In this one respect he was completely obstinate, even when beaten.

After a time he was accepted without further questioning and was given the name Boy-from-nowhere. It was difficult not to like him. He was a happy little fellow, joining at play with the other children of the clan, and even helping in the day's work, which few were prepared to do.

Still, there was something strange about him. He often wandered away on his own, especially at night, when others kept close to the camp fires, fearful of what might be lurking beyond the narrow circle of light. Then suspicion began to dawn. Food supplies were dwindling mysteriously. No matter what was put aside for future use, some always went missing. And more than food. The head man lost a new spear, just after he had completed straightening and polishing the handle and lashing the bone head to the shaft. Another reported the loss of his woomera, while small objects such as gum, bone needles, headbands, and knives were constantly going missing. The only objects that were never taken were those reserved for sacred purposes—tjurunga, the sacred boards, ochre for body painting, pointing bones, and feathered string ropes.

The epidemic of stealing became so serious that the elders kept watch, especially at times when most of the younger men were out of the camp foraging for food. The culprit was soon discovered. The strange boy was seen stealing out of one of the humpies, and was found in possession of a dilly-bag complete with its contents.

A severe beating was a fitting punishment for such a crime, a beating that would put an end to such offences for all time. The boy was held firmly by one of the men while another prepared to administer a thrashing with his spear.

No sooner had he drawn back his arm than something extraordinary happened, something that brought everyone running to see it for himself. The boy had slipped out of his captor's arms and had grown to twice his normal height. He was as tall as the tallest man in the clan.

The man who was about to thrash him let his spear drop from nerveless fingers. The barb fell on the boy's foot, almost pinning it to the ground. Again he doubled in size. He had grown as high as the trees that surrounded the encampment.

This was witchery, devilry. The medicine-man hastened to his hut to prepare spells to drive away the evil spirit that had taken such unusual shape. While he was there the men of the village flung spears at the boy giant. He dodged them adroitly until one, thrown by the most powerful man, penetrated his heart. Like a falling tree, he crashed to the ground and lay still.

Timidly the warriors approached him, looking with awe at the elongated figure, and then with pity as they saw his boyish face.

'We must not bury him,' said the wirinun. 'It would do us much harm if the evil spirit that has possessed this boy were to lie near our camp. It would come out at night, and who knows who the next victim would be?'

'What shall we do with him, then?' someone asked.

'Cover him with bark,' the medicine-man said. 'If we no longer see his face, the good spirits may tell us the meaning of the riddle we have seen today and we shall know how to deal with him.'

Many pieces of bark were needed to cover the corpse, but at last the work was done. Everyone waited for the revelation that was to be made to the medicine-man. And the good spirits found the answer to their problem, for when they raised the bark the following morning, there was no sign of the boy's body. It had vanished during the night.

As the last piece of bark was thrown aside, a tiny four-legged creature with a long tail ran over the stones and hid between them. Its hiding place could not be found; but from then onwards, in that camp, and in many others, small lizards became so common that no one ever remarked on them. Nor did anyone except the wirinun connect them with the boy who had come to the camp as a stranger from nowhere. It must have been that wirinun who passed on the story of the lizard that came from nowhere to others, who told it to those who followed them, so that we may read of it today.

The Meat Ants and the Fire*

There was only one tribe of people in the Dreamtime that knew how fire was made. It was the tribe of the Meat Ants. Ants alone knew the secret of making fire, and if you look at a meat ant you will see that it is indeed the same colour as fire.

In a nearby tribe there lived a young man who had an uncle. One day the uncle went to the mother of the young man and said, 'My nephew will not eat meat we have brought back to the camp. He says that we should eat only the food that has been cooked by fire, for then it will taste better.'

'Fire?' she said wonderingly. 'What is fire? I do not even know if there is such a thing as fire.'

But the young man told his people that there was such a thing as fire. He knew that this was so, for somewhere in the land there was a tribe of people that had been taught how fire was made. He said that if his people would let him go on a long journey he would seek the tribe of people who knew how to make fire. His people said in unison, 'Yes, go out to seek for the people that know how to make fire.'

---

* The legend was collected by the late Miss Mildred Norledge and published in her *Aboriginal Legends from Eastern Australia* (A. H. & A. W. Reed), a collection which was edited and rewritten by the present writer at the suggestion of Emeritus Professor A. P. Elkin. This version of the legend of the Meat Ants is, with some further editing, the same as that included in Miss Norledge's book.

While meat ants should not be included in a collection of stories about lizards, it is hoped that readers will forgive its appearance in this section as there is no special category for the Insect people.

For many days and nights the young man walked across the land. He came across many tribes, but none of them knew how fire was made, nor even what fire was. They sat in darkness when day had ended and night came.

One day the young man saw some children playing, for only the old people and the children were in the camp. The men were out hunting, and the women out gathering food. The young man hoped that they might have the secret, but when night came he knew that these people were also without fire.

He came to another land and although it was forbidden for him to enter it, he looked to the north, and saw a mountain so great that it was like a dividing range across the land. He walked towards it and said to himself, 'If the people who I need do not dwell upon this mountain, then I will return to my own tribe.'

When he came to this mountain he saw children playing together and rolling stones. It seemed to him that these children looked better in stature and countenance than those of his own people and of the other tribes he had seen. It came into his mind that perhaps he had at last found the people whom he had been seeking—the people who knew how fire was made. When he saw the children going up to the peak of the mountain, he said to himself, 'Their camp must be on the peak. I will follow them and see what it is like.'

As he did not wish to be seen, he climbed a tree, walking from tree to tree. So silently and stealthily did he do this that no one saw him, but from the tree tops he was able to watch where the children were going.

When he came to the top of the mountain, he could see the glare of a fire, and knew that at last he had reached his goal.

'Now that I have found what I have been seeking,' he said to himself, 'I must find some way to take fire home to my people.'

There was a grass-tree growing nearby. He cut the tree down to its very roots and took out the core, intending to put a lighted stick of fire inside it as soon as he could get one. He knew very well that these people would not teach him how to make fire, and that to take a burning brand from their fire was the only way he could secure it.

He waited till all the people in the camp were asleep. When he saw no one awake except a little boy, he crept up to him and gave him a stick to play with. The little boy played with this stick and put it in the ashes of the fire until it blazed up. The young man took the stick from the child and thrust it quickly into the core of the grass-tree.

When the boy saw what the young man had done, he ran to where his father lay sleeping and woke him up. In his excitement and fear, the child was unable to speak, but his father at once realised that the boy had seen some strange thing, because he kept pointing to where the young man had gone. All the people in the camp were now awake. They saw the young man's tracks and knew that a stranger had been there.

They followed the young man's tracks and before long he knew that they were on his trail. He found a large vine growing on the mountainside. He slid down it, and when he got close to the root, cut it with his stone axe. The angry tribesmen began to swarm down the vine, not knowing that it had been cut from beneath. The vine gave way as these people took hold of it and they all fell down and were killed.

The courageous young man returned to his own people taking to them the gift of fire, and to the people of other tribes that he met on his way he also gave this gift. In this manner and on that day, fire came to many tribes.

The children of the people from whom the young man took the fire turned into meat ants and meat ants they are to this day. The home of the meat ants is Durundur in the Kabi tribe's country.

CHAPTER TWO

FROG PEOPLE

Many are the tales that are told of the frogs—fables and legends that come mainly but not solely from the well-watered regions of the continent. Like the Aboriginals themselves, frogs have learned to adapt themselves to the most trying climatic conditions. In at least one area of scarce and unreliable rainfall they seem to have foreknowledge of drought conditions. After a fall of rain preceding a long dry period, when water will be no longer available, they fill their bellies until their whole bodies are distended, and bury themselves in the sand. When on walkabout, the Aboriginals of this region are able to detect their presence. They dig the little creatures out of the ground and drink the water imprisoned in the bodies of the frogs.

In the eastern and southern states, the croaking of the frogs reminds them of the gigantic Frog of olden time, known as Tiddalick, Karaknitt, and doubtless many other names. This obese creature is credited with once having swallowed all the water in the region where he lived. It was released only when an ingenious worm succeeded in making him laugh. As the laughter rumbled up from his belly, water gushed out of his mouth, filling rivers, streams, billabongs and waterholes, bringing vegetation to life and quenching the thirst of parched animals and mortals. His laughter continued until the last drop of water was spilt, the sound booming like thunder across the land. He laughed so much that he lost his voice. When he regained it, all he could do was to croak hoarsely with the sound that every frog has since inherited. It may be assumed that the unending chorus of the frogs is an attempt to regain the pleasant tone that was lost by their ancestor when he released the flood water in a gale of laughter.*

---

* The full story of Tiddalick is related in *Myths and Legends of Australia.* Other frog stories appear in *Aboriginal Fables*. Both books by A. W. Reed (A. H. & A. W. Reed).

The Timid Frogs

In striking contrast with the self-assurance of Tiddalick is the size and timidity of the Frogs that inhabit the marshy places of Australia. That they are small in size is of course beyond their control, and indeed an advantage in hiding from their enemies; their timidity, on the other hand, is due to the actions of their male forefathers. It happened that they became so exasperated with their womenfolk that they decided to leave them and form a male community. Nobody knows why. It may be that wives, aunts, sisters, and grandmothers nagged them unmercifully, for this characteristic is not unknown even amongst mortal women, who should have more sense.

In making the momentous decision to leave their comfortable surroundings the male Frogs were as foolish as men who leave their wives. They soon discovered that there was much work to do, day and night, previously performed by the female Frogs, which they had taken for granted.

Nevertheless there were compensations. It was pleasant to sit on the leaf of a waterlily in the evening basking in the last rays of the sun, yarning with friends, with no one to interrupt them, immersing themselves from time to time to keep their skins moist and pliable.

All went well for some time. The male Frogs kept congratulating themselves on their removal from feminine influence, especially in the evenings when the day's hunting was over.

One night there was a strange feeling in the air. No one could describe it or say what it was, but it was felt by everyone. Was it something in the slight breeze from the west? Was it something rustling in the bushes? Did it come from the clouds or was it something moving stealthily under the ground? Or by the pool where they had made their new camp?

It was something they had never felt before. And then they heard it. It was a Voice. Just a Voice. No form, no body, only a Voice. Strong and near and at the same time soft and far away. Not like a man, or an animal, or even a Frog speaking. It came from everywhere, from the sky, and the air, from the water and the ground, from trees and bushes. Some of the Frogs thought it was coming from inside their bodies.

Even stranger, it had no words, and yet they understood what the Voice was saying to them. It was asking for food. The Frogs looked at each other, undecided what to do. How could they possibly give food to a Voice?

The demand from the wordless Voice became imperative. The message it conveyed was that there would be trouble for them if its demands were not satisfied. Hesitantly the Frogs gathered a supply of food and placed it on the margin of the pool. The moon rose and the tiny silver fish they had placed on the bank shone in its rays.

To the astonishment of the Frogs, the fish vanished, one by one. It seemed as though some unseen animal was swallowing them. One of the Frogs, bolder than the others, ventured a question. Jumping on to a fallen tree trunk he said, 'Who are you? We can't see you. What are you?'

The Voice made no reply. The fish had all disappeared. Where they had been lying a little breeze circled round, raising a puff of dust that slowly settled. The brave Frog, who was the leader, hopped closer to examine the ground.

'There are no footprints,' he told the others, who had not ventured near. 'It must have been a ghost, a spirit. Now it has gone.'

The Frogs remained quiet for a long time, expecting to hear the Voice again, but there was no sound except the soft brush of wind against the leaves. The feeling of a presence had gone.

After this experience they were not surprised to feel the unseen visitor and to hear the wordless Voice the following night. Once again they were able to understand its demand for food. Night after night the same thing happened. The invisible creature, if creature it was, had a healthy appetite, and food supplies began to run short.

One morning the leader called the Frogs together.

'This is getting serious,' he said. 'We have no knowledge of what this mysterious visitor is like. He may be as small as a mouse or even a grass-hopper, in which case we have nothing to fear. On the other hand, he may be bigger than an old-man kangaroo. I think we must ask him to show himself to us. Who will volunteer to ask the question?'

No one spoke. The silence became painful. It lasted all day, for in those far-off times Frogs did not speak or croak in their own language as they do today. They took a long time to think before speaking. In this case, however, there was no need for anyone of them to think. They were quite sure it was their leader who would have to face up to the unknown consumer of their food. The leader was well aware that he would have to do it himself.

As evening approached and the strange feeling they had already experienced permeated the Frog people, old-man Frog hopped on to the log, holding tightly to it to still his trembling limbs, and demanded as fiercely as he could that the Voice show himself to them.

'There will be no more food until you reveal yourself.'

No words came from the Voice, only a threatening sound like the distant rumble of thunder, but the Frogs knew instinctively that they were being threatened. Controlling a quaver in his own voice, the Frog leader said again, 'We're not afraid of you. If you can't show yourself to us, at least tell us who you are.'

The message came through clear and strong.

'Tomorrow you will see and hear for yourselves. Watch for my coming when the sun is high in the sky.'

Then there was silence, and a great unease among the Frogs. They could not wait for the appearance of the mysterious creature, yet they were in dread of what might happen. The long night dragged on, and the morning hours. At midday every male Frog kept looking towards the west, standing on the bank or on logs and snags in the pool.

When the sun was overheard they saw a swirling column of dust racing towards them. It was a willywaugh. Was this the Voice? Surely not, for they had all seen willywaughs before. They had no voice, only dust and grit and whirling air and confusion.

It was nearly on them. Its fringe ruffled the water at the end of the pool and once again they were conscious of that menacing Voice that seemed to speak through bone and flesh.

'I ... am ...'—the words came slowly with dreadful meaning and intensity. Before the sentence was completed a hundred bodies dived headlong into the pool. Not one of the Frogs, not even the old-man Frog who had led them, dared stay to hear the name or seek the form from which the wordless Voice was emanating.

To this very day frogs are still in ignorance of the nature of the Voice. They dread the wind that carries sounds on its unseen wings, and that is why they take refuge under water at the slightest noise.

We can only hope that they have become reconciled to their womenfolk, who can offer comfort and tell them how brave they are, even though they know they are the most timid creatures ever created by the Great Spirit of long ago.

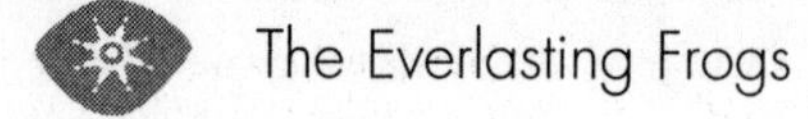

The Everlasting Frogs

For months there had been no rain, but at last dark clouds had banked up from the west, covering the sky. When the sun rose that morning, it sent its fierce rays to beat on the parched earth, turning the last muddy puddle to steam that vanished as quickly as it had been born.

It was scarcely midday. The sun was lost behind the clouds. One of the old women of the tribe peered anxiously through the gloom. She felt a cold wind on her face and the first heavy drops of rain. Amongst the wurleys there was much rejoicing.

'Before the day is over, there will be water in the soak, flowers carpeting the sand, game for the young men to hunt,' the woman's brother said.

'But where are my daughters?' she asked. 'It is two days since they left. They should have returned long since.'

'They have probably gone far into the bush in search of yams and grubs. You know they're hard to find since everything dried up.'

The rain streamed down endlessly. Heat had been eaten up by the cold torrents of water that had soaked into the ground and now lay deep in the hollows, beaten into changing patterns by the drops that fell like spears on the shivering water. Through the night the deluge smashed on the withered branches of the wurleys, penetrating the maze of twigs and leaves, drenching the men and women who crouched beneath them.

In the morning the old woman sought out her brother.

'What of my daughters now?' she asked pitifully. 'Where can they be?'

'Sheltering under a bush, I have no doubt. Soon they will return,' he replied.

Before nightfall the rain had stopped, but there was no sign of the missing girls.

In the morning the distraught mother went to the hump-backed wirinun, the clever-man of the tribe. He, too, was old and surly. In his youth he had desired the woman, but she had refused him. Ever since, he had nourished a grudge and had looked for a way of punishing her.

'I know what you have come for,' he said. 'Nothing is hidden from me. Your daughters are safe.' His laugh was thin and frosty. 'Safe!' he repeated. 'Safer than they had ever been. Safer than they deserve. They are bad women, those girls. They have mocked me, saying that my back is like that of Dinewan the Emu.' He drew himself up as straight as he could. 'Dinewan is my may, my totem. It is not right that they should speak of it so.'

The woman tried to calm him down.

'They were thoughtless, as girls so often are,' she said. 'If they come back they will tell you they are sorry. Now I am frightened, for something terrible may have happened to them. Help me find them.'

'I can help you,' the wirinun said. He pointed to a patch of bush that was darker than the rest, bursting with the new life that had come with the rain. 'Go past the tree that was killed by lightning. Keep straight on, and it may be that you will find them.'

'Or maybe no,' he chuckled to himself as the woman hurried away, splashing through the puddles, her feet brushing heedlessly against the vegetation that had sprung to life so suddenly.

Her spirits lifted as she detected signs of the passing of her daughters. She followed the faint trail hour after hour, unconscious of hunger and thirst, until the rays of the declining sun shining in her eyes warned her that it would soon be night. As darkness fell she curled up at the foot of a gum tree and fell into an uneasy sleep.

In the morning she drank from a pool of water and looked round for something to satisfy her hunger. On the ground, close to the tree, there were signs of the Frogs that shelter in the sand. Scooping the sand up with her hands, she found four Frogs. The thought came into her mind, as though placed there by an unseen spirit, that this was as many as her missing daughters. She put the thought away from her. As she was about to squeeze one of the Frogs to death, in order to eat it, the thought returned with redoubled force. Holding the Frog close to her face, she looked into its eyes. It looked at her so pitifully and seemed to be trying to speak, that she put it down. The little Frog huddled close to the others. All four raised their webbed feet in such a manner that she felt sure they were appealing to her to protect them.

She stepped back, and watched them scuttle into their holes. The croaking of the Frogs sounded almost like words, words that sounded like, 'Thank you, mother.'

The woman sped along the track she had followed so slowly the day before. By midday she reached the cluster of wurleys on the edge of the bush and sought out the hump-backed wirinun.

'What have you done to my daughters?' she demanded.

'So you've found them? I wanted you to see what happens to those who laugh at a wirinun—or to one who refuses to become his wife,' he replied fiercely.

'This is your revenge, then!' the woman said sadly. 'All these years you have harboured these thoughts because I was given to another. My daughters are precious to me. Without them I would starve, for there is no one else to help me now. You know my husband was killed years ago. Was it you who killed him with your evil powers?'

'I shall not tell you, woman. There are many things that wirinun do not reveal.'

'It doesn't matter now,' she said impatiently. 'It is my daughters who are important. The young men will soon be anxious to take them to wife, to bear children, to hunt for yams, to cook their food. The future of our people depends on them. If I come to you now, to be your woman, will you restore my daughters?'

'You are old and wrinkled. The juice has left your body. Your skin is dry and wrinkled. I could have no joy in you now,' the wirinun said contemptuously. 'What else have you to offer besides your body?'

'I have the doori that has come down from father to son for so many generations that the number of them can never be counted. It was the doori that belonged to my husband. I have kept it all these years.'

'The grinding stone that talks when it is fed with seeds!' the wirinun exclaimed, a spark of pleasure kindling in his eyes. 'Yes, I might do something for you and your daughters if you give me your doori.'

The woman hastened to her wurley and brought the grinding stone, laying it at the wirinun's feet.

'Do you promise to restore my daughters to me?' she asked, keeping her hand on it until the wirinun made his promise.

'I promise,' he said, and paused. 'I promise to change your girls. Go back to them. You will see that I keep my promise. They will never be eaten when I have changed them.'

Gleefully he lifted the doori and watched the woman he had deceived running towards the bush and disappearing into the scrub.

It was almost dusk by the time she reached the tree where she had slept during the night. There were no daughters there to greet her—and neither were there any Frogs in the holes close by.

She wondered if her girls were by the pool. Looking frantically in every direction, and calling in a quavering voice, she came to the pool—and there she found her daughters. They had been changed, as the wirinun had promised, but not into living flesh.

By the bank, resting as though they had been drinking the water, were four stones, striped with green, in the shape of Frogs. The promise of that evil man had been fulfilled. Her daughters would never be eaten, for they had been turned to stone.

CHAPTER THREE
TREE PEOPLE

In the beginning all was land. There was no sea. Animals and men were allowed to go wherever they pleased. It was impossible for them to go far, but their children would go a little farther. That is the reason why birds and animals are found in various parts of the continent.

Koala and the Rainbow

It had been raining for days and weeks and months and years. The water ran down the hills, forming creeks and rivers that flowed across the plains and collected in hollows. The water rose almost imperceptibly, lapping gently at the feet of the hills. As the deepest depressions were filled with waters that grew into vast oceans, the land area shrank and divided into many islands. Groups of animals and men were divided from one another by the encircling seas.

On an island far distant from the continent that is now called Australia were men who were skilled throwers of boomerangs. They were able to split a small stone at a hundred paces or more, bring down the swiftest bird in flight, and send their boomerangs so far away that they were lost to sight before returning to the thrower.

They loved to engage in contests of skill to show how far or how accurately they could hurl their weapons. Among them was one who was noted for his strength and also for his boasting.

He was often heard to say, 'If I wished, I could throw my boomerang from here to the most distant of all the islands.'

'If you were able to do that, how would you know whether you had succeeded?' asked one of the more sceptical men.

'The answer to that is simple,' the strong man replied. 'What happens when boomerangs are thrown?'

'They come back to the thrower, of course.'

'What happens if the boomerang hits a tree or a rock?'

'The boomerang stays there, especially if it breaks.'

'You have answered your question,' the strong man said with a grin. 'If I throw my boomerang as far as the farthest island and it fails to return, then you will know I've succeeded, won't you?'

'Yes, I suppose that is so, but what's the use of talking about it unless you actually do it?'

'Very well,' the strong man said. 'Watch.'

He chose a well-balanced boomerang. Whirling it round his head several times, he released it. The weapon flew from his hand so quickly that few could see it as it sped across the ocean. Expectantly the onlookers waited, but as the hours dragged by without any sign of its return, even the old-man sceptic was forced to agree that it might have landed on a distant island.

'But there's another possibility,' he said, annoyed by the way the strong man was strutting to and fro, winning admiring glances from the women. 'It may have landed in the sea.'

'Not my boomerang!' the strong man shouted. 'It would cut its way back to me through the sea if it had not reached the island. You are jealous of my skill, old man.'

'There's only way that we can know for sure,' was the reply. 'Someone must go there to see if he can find it.'

'I know how we can do it,' a small boy piped up.

The old man looked at him disapprovingly.

'We've heard too much from you already,' he growled. 'It would be much better if you ate the food you're given like the other children. I've seen how you spit food out of your mouth—food that's good for you as well as good to eat.'

'That's because no one had ever brought me a Koala to eat. That's what I like best.'

'How can you know you'll like it if you've never tasted it?'

'How do you know there's an island far away over the sea if you've never seen it?' the boy asked cheekily.

'Because I know it's there. It is part of what men who lived and died before I was born have said,' the old man replied.

'I expect they liked Koala meat too,' the boy said. 'My sister's husband caught one this morning. There it is, beside that tree.'

The old man picked up the animal and threw it at the youngster, knocking him over. Picking himself up, he snatched the body of the Koala and ran with it to the beach. Taking a flint knife from the skin girdle he wore, he slit the belly and drew out its intestines. Putting the end in his mouth, he blew into them until they swelled into a long tube that reached the sky. He kept on blowing. The tube bent over in a majestic arch, its end far out of sight beyond the curve of the ocean.

'What are you doing?' the old man asked. 'If you really want to taste the flesh of the Koala, take it to your mother and she will cook it for you.'

'No, no,' exclaimed the boy's brother-in-law. 'Look what he's done. He's made a bridge to the island beyond the sea. Now we can cross it and find where the boomerang had landed. It's sure to be a better place than the one we're living in now.'

He put his foot on the bridge of intestines and began to climb the arch. Next came the boy, followed by his mother's uncle, his father and mother, and aunts and brothers and sisters. Seeing that everyone was crowding on to the bridge of intestines, the old man followed too.

The crossing took many days, days without food and in the burning heat of the sun, but eventually they came to an end of climbing. They slid down the far end of the arch and found themselves on the far away island. It was a good place. The grass was greener than in their own land, shaded by gum trees, with cooler, clearer water than they had ever seen or tasted. And no wonder, for this land to which they had come was the east coast of Australia.

When all the tribespeople were there they let the arched bridge float away. The sun shone on it, turning it to many gleaming colours which formed the first rainbow arch that had ever been seen by men. As they watched the brilliant colours, the rainbow slowly disappeared. The boy was turned into a Koala and his brother-in-law to a Native Cat. Although the other tribesmen remained unchanged, they split up into a number of groups, each with its own totem, and departed to various parts of the island continent. And so it was, said another old man, many generations later, that the first Aboriginals to come from another island became the progenitors of the various tribes which occupied the new land.

Why Koala has no Tail

Koalas were not seen by Europeans until the year 1810. Several theories became current, one being that they were a kind of wombat, another, a type of monkey. Since then much has been learnt about these appealing little creatures. It is known that they were able to survive on the leaves of only twelve varieties of eucalypt, in particular the manna-gum in Victoria, the forest red-gum in New South Wales, and the blue-gum in Queensland. If the water content of the soil changes, the Koala is sometimes forced to frequent a tree of another species. Its capacity for existing with so small an intake of water and relying on gum leaves has naturally given rise to interesting legends (one is related in *Myths and Legends of Australia*).

Another distinguishing feature is its lack of a tail, for which at least two legends provide an explanation.

During a drought the animals noted that Koala never seemed to suffer from thirst. Suspecting that he had concealed a supply of water for his own use and was unwilling to share it with others, they searched high and low. Various birds and animals maintained a watch on his movements day and night, but without success until Lyre-bird saw him scrabbling up a tree and hanging head downwards from one of the branches. In those far-off days Koala was equipped with a tail which proved useful in climbing and allowed him to perform gymnastic feats that his descendants are no longer able to imitate. Curious to know why the little animal had adopted such a curious posture, Lyre-bird crept close. It did not surprise him to find that Koala was sipping water that had collected in the fork of a tree.

It occurred to him that the tree might be hollow and filled with water. As he was unable to reach the branch where Koala was hanging and had no axe with which to fell the tree, he scuttled back to camp and brought a firestick, with which to set the tree alight. The result was spectacular. The trunk burst into little pieces, releasing the water in a miniature torrent. Birds and animals plunged into the water that collected at the foot of the tree and, for the first time in many days, slaked their thirst.

The events of that day left their mark on Lyre-bird and Koala. If one looks closely at the tail feathers of a lyre-bird, it will be seen that there are brown marks on the outer edges where the feathers were scorched by the flaming firestick.

The result of the conflagration had a far more serious effect on Koala. As the flames shot upwards his tail was consumed. He saved himself by scrambling into the branches of an adjacent tree, but ever after he had to learn to live without a tail.

It must be admitted that the legends that have accumulated round Koala belie the apparent lovableness of the Australian teddybear, including the second legend of how Koala lost his tail.

Once again drought had dried up watercourses and ponds. Leaves hung listlessly on the trees, the ground was parched, the grass was dry and brittle. Koala had not yet learned how to survive on gum leaves. In his distress he consulted his friend Tree-Kangaroo.*

'What shall we do?' he asked plaintively. 'Unless the clouds bring rain we shall die of thirst.'

---

* Tree-Kangaroos are found in Queensland. The soles of their feet are rough to prevent slipping on branches, the claws on their fore-paws long and curved, their teeth adapted for eating fruit instead of cropping grass.

Kangaroo leaned back on his long tail and held up his paws.

'We must do something,' he said. 'Let me tell you what happened when I was a very small joey in my mother's pouch. It was a time of drought. There was no water for miles around, and the animals were dying of thirst. Although I was unaware of it at the time, I now know that my mother was thinking more of me than herself. She was fearful I would die too. One morning she said to my father, ''Little Joey will die if we don't get water soon. My milk is dried up. I must find water somewhere.''

'My father gave a harsh croaking laugh. I can hear it still. ''You're a foolish woman,'' he said. ''You know there's no water. All we can do is to shelter under the leafiest part of the trees and hope the rain will come soon.''

'Speaking with difficulty because her tongue was as dry as a piece of old sun-dried skin, my mother said, ''Joey will be dead long before the rain comes. I'm going to take him with me and search for water.''

'''You would suffer far less by remaining here,'' my father warned her. ''Why don't you resign yourself to your fate? Too bad about Joey, but it's not your fault or mine.''

'My mother was a determined woman. She believed that somewhere there must be enough water for me, if not for herself. Remember, Koala, that she was not like the big Kangaroos that roam the plain in great leaps on their strong legs. She was a Tree-Kangaroo like me, made for tree-climbing. As she crept across the dry stubble on the plains and dragged herself painfully over hills and down into dry valleys, her hands and feet grew sore. I must have weighed heavily in her pouch.' He sighed, and went on with his story. 'Her patience and persistence were rewarded. We came to a dried-up watercourse. Even the mud was hard as ironwood, latticed with ugly cracks. She went to where the old stream bed was deepest and began to dig with her poor curved claws. Oh, it was hard work under the burning sun. After a long while she found the soil at the bottom of the hole was damp. And a long while after that, we sat beside the deep hole, waiting for a little water to collect at the bottom. And it did! Only just enough for me, and I drank it. Night fell. I nestled in her pouch. When daylight came there was a pool of water at the bottom of the ditch. Enough for us both; and our lives were saved.'

'Do you know where that pool is?' Koala asked.

'I'm not sure. I think I could find it, but remember, it's not a pool. It will be just a dried-up river bed.'

Koala waved his long bushy tail excitedly.

'What are we waiting for?' he asked. 'I'll help you with the digging. All you have to do is to show me where the water can be found.'

'Very, well,' Tree-Kangaroo replied. 'We'll see if we can find it, but I'll need your help when we get there.'

Like Tree-Kangaroo's mother, the two friends made the long journey in search of the elusive water. After several false alarms they came to a stream bed that Tree-Kangaroo thought he recognised.

'Yes, I'm almost sure this is the place. You'd better have a rest before you start digging, Koala.'

'I don't think we should wait,' said the little Bear, 'but I agree I'm too tired to begin straight away. You look fresher than me. Suppose you take the first spell.'

'Very well,' said Tree-Kangaroo.

He had already said this several times on the journey when Koala had asked him to forage for food, and felt it was becoming his least favourite expression.

He scratched the hard surface of the river bed and dug quickly down to the softer soil below. Presently he stopped and said, 'It's your turn now, Koala'—but Koala was no longer there. He was lying in the shade under the wilting trees, fast asleep. He looked so helpless and pathetic with his tail draped across his face and his tiny paws clasped, that Tree-Kangaroo took pity on him and went on digging.

Several times he went back to ask Koala to take his turn but on each occasion he was either asleep or had some excuse, such as a thorn in his paw, or cramp in his leg. Tree-Kangaroo grew more and more exasperated.

'You're just plain lazy expecting me to do all the work,' he complained. 'If you don't do your part I'll not let you have the water. It's not far off now. In a little while we'll come to it.'

'I wouldn't deprive you of the privilege of finding it,' Koala said. 'Not now, after all you've done. I'll go and see if I can find something to eat.'

He trotted off into the trees while Tree-Kangaroo returned wearily to the hole. His claws were blunt and every movement was agony. He seethed with anger as he thought how selfish his friend had been. But at that moment he saw a trickle of water at the bottom of the hole. His resentment vanished in the excitement of the find. He jumped out and called, 'Here it is! Water! I've found it at last!'

Koala had deceived his friend. He had not attempted to search for food. Once Tree-Kangaroo's back was turned he had tiptoed to the edge of the bush. As soon as he heard the shout of triumph, he rushed over to the hole, pushed Tree-Kangaroo aside, dived in head-first, and began to lap the water.

Tree-Kangaroo was furious. That greedy, selfish Koala was drinking the water he had worked to uncover without lending hand or paw to help. There was no sign of Koala except for his long brush tail standing straight out of the hole like a grass-tree. He bent down and with one short, sharp snap of his strong teeth, he severed the tail at the base. It fell limpy on the river bed—and that is how Koala lost his tail, for ever and ever.

Man into Possum

The first Possum that ever lived began life as a man. The story begins with two brothers who were expert fishermen. They were dissatisfied with the methods adopted by other fishermen and invented several ingenious devices. Long before the first bark or dug-out canoe had been invented, they used a log to take them to the best fishing ground in the lagoon near their home.

Their canoe was roughly boat-shaped, partly hollowed out by fire, partly by adze or axe, to provide a comfortable place in which to sit. It was a crazy craft, liable to turn over at any moment. Forced to spend hours at a time trying to catch fish with their primitive hooks, the brothers often complained at the heat of the sun.

At the front end of the log, in the position that later men termed the bow, there was a long crack. One of the brothers thought about it a great deal, wondering whether some use could be made of it. It was on a day of burning sunshine that a thought was born. When the log was brought ashore at the end of the day's fishing, he pulled a leafy bough off an overhanging tree and forced the butt into the crack.

'What's that for?' his brother asked. 'The log will turn over if you leave it there.'

'Not so,' the other replied. 'Don't you see it is quite light? The leaves will protect us from the fierce sunlight. We'll be as cool sitting on the logs as if we were resting under the trees.'

His brother agreed it was worth trying. When they set out for the fishing ground the following morning, working with the roughly shaped paddles that usually moved the log sluggishly across the water, they were surprised to find that they were travelling much faster than they expected.

'It's the branch,' one of them said, his voice raised in excitement. 'The wind is blowing against it and pushing us across the water. We won't be tired before the day's work is done.'

It was a momentous discovery, but there were drawbacks as well as advantages. When the wind changed during the day and helped to blow them back at night, all was well; but if the wind blew constantly it proved necessary to take the leafy branch down and throw it away. The constant placing of branches and removing them wore a part of the crack so smooth that it was difficult to wedge them in securely. They hammered in a thick piece of wood to support the makeshift sail; and when they found how to tie the branch to the side of the log when it was not needed, they no longer had to find a suitable replacement every day.

The next problem arose when the leaves withered.

'I know,' one brother said. 'Let's weave pandanus leaves through the twigs. It doesn't matter if they dry in the wind.'

Shortly after this a peculiar thing happened. They were nearly home, making good time with a strong breeze behind them, when a sudden gust of wind tore the branch from the log. Before they could reach it the river swept it out of sight.

It doesn't matter, they thought. It's bound to land up on the bank. We'll fetch it back in the morning. That is just what happened. The branch had caught on a snag close to the bank. It swung round in the current with the woven sail downstream. Caught in the coarse mesh of the makeshift sail were several fair-sized fish. Unknown to themselves, the brothers had invented the first fishing net!

After this they were noted as the best fishermen in the world. With a net, as well as with lines and hooks, they kept the whole clan supplied with fish, and often had enough over to barter with less fortunate clans.

Close to the camp there was a small salt-water pond. A narrow channel linked it with the lagoon, and the water in the pool rose and fell with the tide. It proved an excellent place in which to keep surplus fish alive, ready for bartering with other family groups in the vicinity.

One day a stranger came into their district, unseen by anyone in the village. He was a cunning man who lived a lonely life, keeping himself alive by stealing food wherever he could find it. Hearing sounds of men and women at work on the morning of his arrival, he concealed himself among the trees. As he stood there he heard splashing sounds as though someone was hitting the water with a hand or a paddle. Making his way cautiously towards the sound, he came to the pool and looked with astonishment at the fish leaping and falling back into the water. There seemed to be hundreds of them. He saw the little channel leading to the lagoon and wondered why they did not escape. Closer inspection revealed a lattice work of crossed sticks that the fishermen brothers had placed across the mouth of the channel to keep the fish penned up in the pool.

The stranger then realised the purpose of the fish pen. He rubbed his hands in delight, thinking no one would ever miss the few he would take, and that he need have no worries about food shortages for a long while, provided he was careful to let no one see him at work.

For many days he remained concealed, helping himself to the fish as he needed them, and on one or two occasions carrying a number of them to a distant encampment where he exchanged them for other provisions.

The fishermen had a method of placing the catch in a basket tied to a log. The basket was kept in the water so that the fish could be placed in the pond alive.

But there were no fish to put in the pond. The arrival of the stranger coincided with a lean period for the fishermen. In spite of all their efforts day after day they returned without a single fish. The villagers were puzzled. The fish population of the holding pen was being depleted more rapidly than expected. No one could tell why, until the inventive brothers decided to keep watch.

It was early in the morning when they found the culprit. He was scooping the fish up in his hands and throwing them into a basket. Seeing the brothers rushing towards him, brandishing their clubs, he looked round, seeking somewhere to escape. The brothers came at him from opposite directions. The fish pond was in front of him, and behind him a tall tree, too smooth-barked for a man to climb.

In desperation he remembered a magic spell he had learned long ago. He spoke it aloud. He grew smaller, claws grew out of his fingers, his skin was covered with fur, and his spear turned into a tail. Like a flash of lightning he scaled the tree, clinging to the branches with tail and claws. The brothers had witnessed the transformation. They too knew a spell, that prevented the thief from changing back into a man.

So the solitary fish thief became a Possum, a Possum whose children and children's children are thieves who sneak into the encampments of men at night to rob them of food.

Red and Black Flying-foxes

When one of Captain Cook's men saw a flying fox in 1770 he was frightened out of his wits, thinking he had seen a real devil. The large 'fruit bats' have a wing span of a metre or more and would certainly appear to be a gruesome apparition at first sight. Contrary to what might be thought, their natural food is flowers, with fruit a secondary item of diet. Nevertheless enormous 'camps' containing a hundred thousand or more flower-eating bats can do irreparable damage to fruit trees. They are quarrelsome animals, a trait which is clearly brought out in a Queensland legend.

The tale begins with a quarrel between two men, one of whom belonged to the red Flying-fox totem, the other to the black. As related by a member of the Munkan tribe, there is a full description of how these early men of the red Flying-fox totem made spears. 'They used to fasten the ''nose'' of the spear-thrower with gum, and, cutting a baler shell, would put the pieces on with beeswax. They used a small spear, a *pepin*, with a wooden point and no barb. They also cut acacia wood, whittled down the four wooden prongs, and fastened them on with gum. They shaped bone barbs, planing them on a flat palette, fastening them with string made of fig tree fibre. They smeared their spears with red clay, and put on white paint with the finger. Then they carried them on their shoulders.'

In recording the fireside tale as related by a man of the Munkan, Ursula McConnel in *Myths of the Munkan* explains the symbolism of the spear and the action of the story.* 'It has many interesting features: the transformation of the *pulwaiya* (totemic ancestor) into the flying-fox is appropriate on account of the quarrelsome nature of the flying-fox, which also makes them an excellent subject for the depiction of a merciless vendetta, such as may occur in real life, even severing family relationships. The way flying-foxes hook on to fig trees is sufficient to explain their manufacture here of the spear-thrower, with its hook at one end, and the pronged spear, the barbs

* Included by permission of Melbourne University Press.

of which are fastened with the fibre of the fig tree on which the flying-foxes camp …

'The manner of burial described is that of cooking the flying-fox, i.e. digging a hole, laying ant-bed and covering it over with tea-tree bark. This story contains the only reference in these parts to the funeral custom, common elsewhere, of standing up grave sticks decorated with feathers.'

In the light of these valuable comments the story takes on new meaning.

The Red Flying-fox men were quarrelling among themselves and throwing spears at one another. One of the spears thrown by the father Flying-fox, Wuka, went wide and entered the leg of Mukama who belonged to the Black Flying-fox clan. Fighting stopped at once. Wuka went up to Mukama and put out his leg, saying, 'Here is my leg. Spear it,' to put an end to any further reprisals. Mukama's spear, however, entered the leg of a younger brother, also named Wuka (which was evidently a generic name for the family or clan). Both Mukama and Wuka were sick from the wounds they had received, but Mukama recovered, while Wuka died. So began the vendetta between the red and black clans.

Mukama's brothers taunted their enemies.

'See if you can spear our younger brother in the leg too! We have plenty more brothers to avenge him.'

There followed much wounding by spears.

The body of the dead Wuka was ceremonially burnt. Tea-tree bark was placed over the remains with were covered with sand—the method employed by the Aboriginals to cook flying-foxes. Sticks were placed in the ground by the grave and decorated with layers of Jabiru and Emu feathers.

While the funeral ceremonies were being performed, Mukama the elder carried the wounded Mukama away and lowered him to the ground; but no sooner was this done than the elder Wuka bounded across and pinned him to the ground with his spear, killing him instantly.

The conflict was renewed. This time it was a still younger Wuka who was killed, and so ended this particular vendetta, though it did nothing to stop further feuds between the two clans. As the blood of the young Wuka dropped on the ground and soaked into it, it softened the soil. All the Flying-foxes sank into it, black and red alike, through the earth and into the water that is dyed red with the blood of Wuka.

For the Aboriginals of those parts good came of the conflict. They strike the water with their hands and say, 'May there be plenty of red flying-foxes soon everywhere,' and their wish comes true, for the trees are laden with the clinging flying-foxes that are cooked in ant-beds and provide good eating for the men and women of Queensland.

CHAPTER FOUR

ANIMAL PEOPLE

One legend antedates all others in describing how animals came to Australia. Long before there were any four-footed animals in this country, flocks of birds migrated from distant lands. Theirs was a reconnaissance flight. On their return they reported on the quality of the great island continent.

'It has vast open spaces, dense forests, mountain ranges, lakes, rivers, stony deserts. There is room for every kind of animal,' they said. 'Trees for Possums and Koalas, deserts and grassland for Kangaroos and Wallabies, soft earth for Wombats to dig burrows, streams for Platypuses, something for everyone.'

On hearing this the animals held a corroboree, during which they decided to emigrate to the new land. There was only one problem—how to get there. They had no canoes and, unlike the birds, were unable to take to the air. Then someone remembered that Whale had a canoe that was large enough to take all the animals. Would he lend it to them?

'No,' said Whale irritably. He had no love for his fellow animals who lived on land and had no need to keep coming up for air.

It was the gallant Starfish who proved to be the hero of the occasion. He persuaded Whale to lie down while he scraped the barnacles from his skin. Whale found the experience so soothing that he fell asleep. As soon as Starfish assured them that the leviathan was asleep, the animals launched the canoe, scrambled into it, and paddled for their lives in order to get as far from land as possible before Whale awoke.

When at last he did wake from sleep and discovered that his cherished canoe was missing, his fury knew no bounds. He picked Starfish up and pulled him to pieces—which explains why the poor little creature is now such a strange shape. It only took a moment before the huge mammal set off in pursuit of his canoe. The animals had a long start. When they flagged in their efforts at the paddles Koala encouraged them, setting an example by paddling even faster, and they managed to reach the entrance to Lake Illawarra in advance of Whale. It was touch and go, but they made it! Running the canoe on to the land, they leapt ashore and scampered off to different parts of the continent, each choosing the type of country that suited him or her best.

All of which explains why different animals are found in different parts of Australia—and why Whales swim up and down the east coast, still trying to catch up with them.

The Legs of the Kangaroo

Of all the animals, the kangaroo may be regarded as the most important as a source of food. Its unusual gait provided inspiration for dancers. There is a legend that tells how a Kangaroo, watching the dancers at a corroboree from behind a tree, was so carried away by the rhythm that he could not refrain from joining in. When the performers had recovered from their stupefaction at such an unusual intrusion they entered into the spirit of the occasion. Rolls of skin were tied to their girdles in imitation of the tail, and they began to hop in a circle with the Kangaroo. So the Kangaroo Dance was born.

But as the Kangaroo had intruded into the semi-sacred mystery, it became necessary to regularise the situation; the elders permitted him to join the candidates at the initiation ceremony, a privilege accorded no other animal. It will be seen that a situation of this kind would be connected in some way with the totemic applications of a particular moiety.

Many are the legends connected with this unique animal. When it arrived in Australia with its companions on the canoe of the Whale its legs were uniform in length. It walked on all four legs, as a dingo walks. One generation was succeeded by another, and still the Kangaroo browsed on the plains, using his legs in the normal manner. Then came Man the hunter, eager for meat, with threatening spear-thrower and spear that could travel faster than any four-legged animal.

Kangaroo was resting in the shade of a tree when his sensitive ears picked up the sound of something approaching stealthily. He bounded to his feet and saw it was a Man—and that Man had a weapon against which he was defenceless. The only thing to do was to take refuge in flight. Kangaroo had seen that the strange creature threatening him with a throwing implement had only two legs. He felt confident that his four legs would carry him out of danger without difficulty.

He had underestimated his enemy. Man proved swift and strong. His two legs were longer than Kangaroo's four legs, and more strongly muscled. They carried Man tirelessly for hour after hour. No matter how he extended himself, Kangaroo was unable to increase his lead. He was saved only by the setting sun and the darkness that fell on the earth. Exhausted by his exertions, Kangaroo fell wearily to the ground.

Presently he lifted his head. A bright light had appeared in the darkness. Man had kindled a fire to warm himself in the cold night air. Cautiously Kangaroo edged back, rose to his feet, and tiptoed away from the revealing light of the camp fire. In order to make no sound, he rose on his hind legs and in this manner managed to escape. Presently he realised that he was using only two legs instead of four, just as Man had done during the long pursuit. It was an unusual sensation. He experimented further, and found he could cover the ground more quickly by hopping instead of walking or running. Using his tail to balance himself, he was able to leap further, much further than a Man could stride.

It was such an exhilarating experience that he has kept on doing it ever since. His forelegs and paws were of little use. They grew smaller, while his hind legs grew longer and stronger, and they have remained like that to this very day.

The Mice Women who Turned into Dingoes

Pungalung was the biggest hunter who ever lived. If you had seen him you would have called him a giant. He lived in the centre, not far from Ayers Rock. In those days there were no hills. If there had been, you would have seen that he was as high as the hills. Even higher. He was so big that when he killed a kangaroo, he tucked its head under his waist-girdle and let it hang there. His nulla-nulla was as large as a tree. When he walked the ground shook.

Everyone was afraid of Pungalung. Especially women, for he was a woman hunter as well as a hunter of animals. Because of his size Pungalung was able to travel long distances. In a single day he could visit places that most families had not seen, even on walkabout. Pungalung enjoyed these long excursions, for he saw places and people that no one else had ever visited.

One of the strangest things he ever saw was the Mice Women who lived far away. They were all women. There were no men in their tribe. They had never seen a man, so when Pungalung came striding across the desert to their camp, they ran about, looking at him and wondering who and what he was.

Pungalung bent down to look at them.

'Are there no men in your tribe?' he asked in his booming voice. 'Where have they gone?'

'We didn't know what men were like until we saw you,' said one of the Mice Women, who was the leader of the tribe. She was bigger and taller than any of the women.

'Then I will show you what a Man is like,' Pungalung said and held out his arms, expecting her to come to him.

The Mice Woman drew back. She was puzzled and a little afraid of what might happen next. Pungalung caught her round the waist and drew her to him. At last the Mice Woman knew what a man was like, and what men did to women! She screamed and bit him on the lip. At the same time all the Mice Women started shouting, trying to make Pungalung release their leader. Their shouts were only squeaks, but they startled the giant.

The Mice Women kept on shouting. Their voices grew deeper and sounded more like growls and barks than squeaks. The women grew bigger. They changed from Mice to Dingoes. They bared their teeth and snapped at Pungalung. He threw their leader from him, and stood up, holding his club ready to ward them off. By this time the Dingoes had become bold. One of them fastened her teeth in Pungalung's leg. He tried to shake her off, but as he did so another caught hold of his other leg. A third Dingo leapt at his throat.

Nothing like this had ever happened to Pungalung. It had been so easy for him to knock down kangaroos and wallabies and emus with club or spear. It was something quite different to be attacked by a pack of Dingoes. He turned and ran.

No matter how fast he ran the Dingoes followed close behind, snapping at his heels. Dropping all his weapons, he made a spurt and managed to increase the distance between himself and the racing Dingoes, but he knew they would soon catch up with him. Not far ahead there was a tree. He ran to it, pulled it up by the roots, ran his hands down the trunk to rub off the branches, and bent it into the shape of a boomerang. He felt more confident with a weapon again in his hands, and turned to face the pack.

Swinging the roughly-made boomerang at the nearest dingo, he knocked out its teeth. It was a grand fight while it lasted. There were times when Pungalung was nearly buried under a snarling mass of Dingoes, but after a while he got the better of them. One by one he smashed his boomerang into their faces and knocked out their teeth, until the last of the toothless Dingoes turned and ran off to nurse its wounds.

No one knows what happened to them. Perhaps they turned back to Mice Women again. If that is so we can be sure they would have nothing to do with Men. And we can be even more sure that Pungalung kept well away from Mice Women. He had barely escaped with his life, and was bleeding profusely from a hundred Dingo bites.

In fact, little is known of what Pungalung, the great hunter and woman chaser, did after the day when he was attacked by the Mice Women. All we know for certain is that the hills that grew out of the plain are the heads of animals he killed, and that he slipped and fell between two of these same hills. The huge boulders that lie at their foot are the bones of the giant Pungalung who barely escaped with his life from the Mice Women.

The Two Dogs

Long ago an old man and his nephew lived on a plateau in the McPherson Range where the north-eastern border of New South Wales meets the south-eastern border of Queensland. They had no other relatives, and lived alone except for their dogs, who were called Burrajahnee and Inneroogun.

One day the dogs chased a kangaroo which fled from the plateau down the steep mountainside. The old man and his nephew feared that the dogs might be lost to them in the excitement of the chase. They called repeatedly, but the dogs took no notice.

The men who lived in the foothills had also seen the chase. Although they had never had an opportunity of seeing them, they had heard of the fame of Burrajahnee and Inneroogun, who were noted hunting dogs, and realised what an unusual opportunity it was to capture them as well as a kangaroo.

The kangaroo had chosen a well-defined path that led from the mountainside to the lagoon near the camping ground of these people. They placed two nets across the track, slinging them between trees, and stood back to see what happened. The kangaroo was unable to stop when it got to the first net. It hurled itself at it and broke through the flimsy meshes. When it came to the second net, which had been placed close to the bank of the lagoon, it leapt high into the air, clearing the net, and plunged head first into the water where, it is said, it turned into a bunyip, which preyed on people who came to live by the lagoon in later years.

The dogs were close on the kangaroo's tail. Passing through the torn net they became entangled in the folds of the second one by the lagoon.

The men who had failed to catch the kangaroo said, 'Oh well, the dogs will serve as well. They will make just as good eating as the kangaroo.'

The tribeswomen prepared an oven while the men killed and skinned the dogs. The feast that night was followed by a dance, and sound sleep for all who had filled their bellies with the unusual food. It was a sleep from which they never woke.

High up on the plateau two lonely men called to their dogs in vain.

'Burrajahnee! Inneroogun!' they called over and over again, but no answering bark came back from the lowlands.

When night fell the men descended from the plateau and crept stealthily towards the faint glow from the embers of the camp fire. They saw the prone figures of men and women and children—and the tell-tale pile of bones of their greatly loved dogs. With hearts swollen with anger, the older man promised a terrible revenge on those who had stolen Burrajahnee and Inneroogun simply to satisfy their appetites. The uncle and nephew gathered the bones together, moving softly so as not to disturb the sleepers, wrapped the bones in bark, and reverently carried them back to the plateau. When any of the bones, such as a foreleg or foot, fell off as they climbed the steep valleys, the place where it fell was named after that bone, and so the name remains to this day.

On the way they came to a waterfall where they sat down to rest, placing their burdens on the ground. The old man faced in one direction, his nephew in the other; and there the remains of Burrajahnee and Inneroogun were turned to stone. The stone dogs are still to be seen at the top of the waterfall, facing in opposite directions.

The stone dogs are sacred. No man dares to touch them.

As for those who killed them and ate their flesh, they vanished from the face of the earth. The last act of the old man who loved his dogs was to conjure up a great wind that blew them all away—so far that they were never seen again.

Water-rat and Fire

There was a time, which lasted many ages, when man lacked the most valued gift that mankind has ever known, the gift of fire. Strange to tell, it was discovered by Water-rat of all people! Before his epoch-making discovery, men lived a miserable existence, eating food of every kind raw and shivering in their makeshift shelters on winter nights.

Amongst those who suffered in this way were Water-rat and his wife. Life went on pleasantly enough in summer, but in winter, after spending some hours foraging for food in the billabong where he lived, Water-rat would creep through the tunnel that led to his burrow, soaked to the skin and feeling as miserable as only a Water-rat can feel.

The only way he could get any warmth into his flesh and bones was to snuggle close to his wife, an attention she failed to appreciate. And this was not the only thing she complained about. Their home was too small, especially now that the family was increasing. In summer it was hot and stuffy. In winter a dank wind blew through the tunnel from the billabong, penetrating every corner.

'We need a larger home,' she kept saying. 'Why don't you make another tunnel with a room at the end where the wind won't whistle round it? I can't keep anything dry where we are. When you come in from food gathering, water gets everywhere and makes puddles on the floor. Look, there's mud everywhere you've been walking.'

Water-rat was disinclined for the hard work entailed in digging a tunnel and constructing an annexe to his burrow. It was all very well in his courting days, when he was young and strong, but now he was older and most of the day was taken up in feeding a brood of young Water-rats.

Constant nagging by his wife at last drove him to it. From then on he was the one who did most of the complaining. The further he got from the soft soil of the bank, the harder it became, and full of rocks. When he came to the roots of a tree, he was ready to give up, but his wife pointed out that it would be a pity to waste all his work.

One day he backed out of the tunnel in sudden alarm.

'A strange thing has happened,' he said. 'I was gnawing at the root when my teeth slipped and I bit into a stone. There was a flash of light. What do you think could have happened? What could it have been?'

'Imagination,' his wife said shortly, thinking it was only an excuse to stop work.

It was not imagination, for as he went on with his work, the same thing occurred several times. On each occasion it was when his teeth closed on a stone.

'It's a very strange thing about the lights that come and go so quickly,' he said one night. 'I can't understand it. One of the lights fell on my paw today and it was hot. It burnt my fur. I could smell it. I wonder what it is.'

The sparks struck from his teeth had set him thinking. 'If I could make them last longer instead of dying as soon as they are born, we could light up our burrow and make it warm,' he told his wife.

He thought about it for a long time. One night he dreamed that the burrow was flooded with light as though the sun was shining inside it, and that bright red and yellow spirits were leaping up from a pile of sticks on the floor. Strangest of all, his wife and children were holding their paws out to the leaping spirits, and steam was rising from their fur. A word came into his mind. It was the word that Water-rats afterwards used for Fire when it raced through the bush and sent them scurrying into their burrows.

When he woke he wondered whether there was some way of summoning the fire spirits. He remembered that the tiny baby spirits that were born and died in an instant appeared when he bit accidentally into a rock. Back in the dark tunnel he clamped his teeth against a stone and once again a spark appeared. Holding a stone in his paws, he struck it against a rock face and a shower of sparks flew out.

'They die too quickly,' he thought. 'Is there a way to make them live?'

Night after night he experimented in the burrow, striking one thing after another against stones he had dug out of the tunnel.

'I wonder if there's another way,' he reflected. He looked round. In the corner were two pieces of wood that had been floating on the water of the billabong. They were quite dry. One was flat, the other was a stick, pointed at one end. He set it upright on the wood and twirled it between his paws. Presently a tiny wisp of smoke rose from the flat pieces of wood. He scattered dry grass on it and kept on turning the stick in his paws, pressing it against the base piece.

With a shock he realised that the baby spark spirits were gathering in the grass. He blew on them and suddenly, in the smoke, the flame spirits came to life. Water-rat had discovered the secret of fire. There was great rejoicing in the burrow that night. The family was sitting round the fire, warming themselves and watching the dance of the shining spirits. Every night the family went to sleep warm and well fed, for they had also discovered the art of cooking food.

But as summer came, the Water-rat woman resumed her complaints. 'It's so smoky inside that I can hardly breathe,' she said. 'Why don't you take the flame spirits outside?'

As the days were growing longer and warmer, Water-rat agreed. Taking his apparatus on to the bank, he kindled a fire. He was glad when his wife appeared satisfied with an outdoor meal.

As night fell, wide-eyed animals of every kind gathered round, watching the flame spirits. Water-rat saw the reflection of the flames in their eyes and hastily extinguished the fire.

In time the animals became bolder. They saw how much better food must be if it were cooked by the spirits of the flame that provided heat as well as light. They begged Water-rat to give them some of the fire. Water-rat at heart was a very selfish animal. He kept the fire to himself and his family and refused to tell the secret to anyone.

The other animals tried to take it from him by force, but Water-rat was too wily. As soon as he saw them coming, he poured water on the fire. They resorted to stealth. Animals of every kind tried to steal the fire. Tortoises crawled through the long grass, large animals like the kangaroo jumped out unexpectedly, small birds flew past trying to snatch a piece of the fire, but all in vain.

When every attempt had failed, the animals ventured to approach Eagle-hawk, who was usually too proud to associate with earth-bound creatures. They told him what they wanted and asked him to help.

'Yes,' he said reflectively. 'I have seen this fire of Water-rat and wondered what it was. From what you tell me, it could be very useful. You've been going about it all the wrong way. Leave it to me.'

He soared up into the sky on his powerful wings until he was lost to sight; but he, the great Eagle-hawk, could see the ground far below and everything on it. He saw Bower-bird building its mound, the waterlilies floating on the billabong, Brown Snake gliding through the grass stalking a small animal, and Water-rat coming out of his burrow and swimming across the water.

With spread wings he floated down through the air and fell like a thunderbolt on the startled Water-rat. Sharp claws dug into his back and Water-rat felt himself lifted up, far from the earth. It was a frightening experience for an animal of land and water. Even more frightening was the thought that Eagle-hawk would feed him to his fledglings. He begged to be released, promising anything that Eagle-hawk wanted if only he would return him to earth.

'If I open my claws, you'll return to earth more quickly than you want, Water-rat,' Eagle-hawk said with a touch of humour. 'There's nothing you can give me that I want, but you can do something for your fellow animals down below. You know how much they want to share the fire you've discovered. Promise me you'll give it to them and I'll set you down by your own home. But if you try to cheat and keep the fire to yourself you'll come with me for another journey in the sky. That journey will have a different ending. I'll drop you like a stone.'

Water-rat was only too anxious to make the promise, and for fear of what might happen he kept it faithfully.

The gift of fire has been known to men for so long that most of them have forgotten that it was first discovered by Water-rat; but selfishness is not quickly forgotten, and Water-rat has never since been popular, either with men or animals.

Echidna's Spines

Several stories have been invented to account for the spines of the echidna. Perhaps there were once as many legends as there were tribes, all of them having much the same origin but with varying details.

In one of the legends, Echidna seemed to be thriving while all the other animals were dying of thirst. As happened in the case of Koala in another legend, everyone believed that Echidna had a secret store of water and that he was keeping it for himself.

Bimba-towera, the Finch, was told to follow Echidna wherever he went, to find the location of the hidden reservoir.

'But he'll see me,' Bimba protested. 'He won't go near the water if he sees I'm watching him.'

'Sooner or later he must drink,' they told him. 'He can't go without water for ever. That's when you'll find where he keeps it.'

Bimba followed his instructions. Everywhere that Echidna went, Bimba was close behind. The wily little Ant-eater knew very well why he was being followed. He said nothing but began to burrow into the earth with his strong claws. Soon he was lost to sight. Bimba cautiously put his head into the hole but withdrew it in alarm as the soil collapsed.

He reported his failure to the animals, who were at a loss to know what to do next. Not one of them was equipped for burrowing beneath the earth, and it looked as though Echidna would keep his secret while everyone else perished.

Then Tiddalick the Frog offered to help. He was a cunning fellow. He has shrunk in size since the day he had swallowed all the water in the land and then disgorged it (see page 30), and had been thirsty ever since. He was as eager to find where Echidna kept the water as anyone, and much more cunning than Bimba in concealing his movements.

He made no attempt to follow the Ant-eater, but browsed among the reeds, taking no notice of Echidna. For most of the time his back was turned. Seizing his opportunity while Tiddalick seemed to be engrossed in catching a fly, Echidna darted to his waterhole. It was concealed by a large flat stone, which he lifted prepared to lower himself into the depression.

In spite of his apparent inattention, Tiddalick had been watching Echidna's every move. Immediately the stone was raised, he covered the intervening distance in a single bound, and dropped head-first into the hole.

Echidna started back as the water splashed up on to his face.

'What are you doing here?' Tiddalick asked before Echidna had time to open his mouth. 'This waterhole belongs to all the animals. You have no right to come sneaking up and stealing it when we're not looking.'

But this time all the animals had arrived. The first thing they did was to slake their thirst, after which they turned on Echidna and threw him into a thorn bush. When they left Echidna dragged himself free, but was never able to remove the spines from his back.

In another legend Echidna was an old man who lived with his wife in a humpy. He was the mystery man of the tribe, for he was never seen. His wife, who was much younger, mixed with the other women and took her part in food-gathering and cooking. She shared meals with others but had never been seen to take food to the hut she occupied with her husband. Indeed, she had not been near him for longer than anyone could remember. To all questions she made no reply, except to say that what her husband did was her husband's business, and that if they wanted to, they were welcome to ask him.

A much greater problem was vexing the tribe. Every new moon one of the young men of the tribe disappeared, never to return. It was not for many moons that anyone thought to connect the old man, who never ate or showed himself to others, with the fate of the young men. The possibility of there being some connection was raised at a council meeting of the elders. Heads were shaken, for everyone knew the solitary hermit was indeed very old and probably feeble. But at least it was worth investigating. At the conclusion of the meeting the elders took their spears and advanced in a body to the bark hut that had been set up at a distance from the other humpies.

They were horrified at what they saw. The old man was sitting on a pile of human bones, gnawing the meat from a thigh bone. They dragged him out of his hut and stabbed him again and again with their spears, leaving them protruding from his back. By the time they left his arms and legs were broken and his back a mass of bristling spears. He crawled into the undergrowth and was never seen again—unless by any chance that strange animal with deformed legs and feet, with a mass of bristling spines on his back, happened to be that old man!

When his wife, who belonged to the totem of the Robin, heard what her husband had done and of his awful fate, she struck her head with a tomahawk till the blood flowed down her face and breast. And from then onwards the Robin has displayed a red breast in remembrance of that day of horrors.

CHAPTER FIVE

FLOWER PEOPLE

There is a sense in which Aboriginal legends may be regarded as utilitarian. Life depended on fresh water and food, and so natural elements of rain and storm, sunlight and shadow, together with earth, sea and sky, and the Great Spirit who brought them to life, were important, each of them having stories of how it came into being or how it attained its present form. For another reason too, animals had more than a fair share of imaginative conjecture and belief attached to them, for every man had a direct affinity with the animal that in turn represented his totemic ancestor. Of flowers, and the beauty of flowers, Aboriginal man had little to say. He was too busy keeping body and soul together to notice the miracle of plant life, except for yams and berries, and grass seed that was ground to make cakes in the embers of the fire. It is pleasing, therefore, to know that the gentler aspects of life were mentioned in legends where flowering plants were personified.

As might be expected, many legends are connected with food and its gathering. The story of the blue Waterlily family from Cape York Peninsula comes into this category. In order to appreciate it fully some knowledge of the plant is necessary. The legend was collected by Ursula McConnel and included in her *Myths of the Munkan*. In relating it as told to her by a member of the Wik-kalkan tribe, she prefaces it with the following explanation:

'When the waterlilies first appear above water, the Waterlily people gather the first roots and cook them in an ant-bed near the *auwa* of the waterlily *pulwaiya* and leave them there uneaten to be washed away by the floods. By this ritual of cooking the first waterlily roots, they remember their *pulwaiya*, the first Waterlily family, and this ensures a plentiful supply of waterlily food for the coming season.

'The flood waters carry the old roots out to sea, but the strong young roots stay in the ground near their old ''Camp''; the seeds are carried everywhere into lagoons and creeks.'

The author goes on to explain that the name for the whole plant is often applied to the root, which provided food and is therefore regarded as the most important part of the plant. Each part of the waterlily plant has its own use, and is regarded as a member of a family, the flower and seed-pod being the father,* the main root the mother, the tender young roots the childen, the short stalk that bears the bud the eldest son. The little roots surrounding the mother root are the as yet unborn babies.

Coral Creeper

Yoondalong had been promised to the old man Yebblegoot as soon as she was born. When she was old enough to know her fate, she dreaded the day when her initiation ceremonies would be completed and she would be taken by the old man. By then, she thought, he would be older and uglier than he was now. She was told that at the age of sixteen she would be ready to mate with Yebblegoot, who already had two wives, but relished the thought of taking a fresh young girl into his family.

Like many another girl, Yoonda wished that she was free to marry a younger man, but it was useless to hope for such a happy event. Yebblegoot had performed his part of the bargain by supplying her parents with food for several years. There was only one person in the group who shared Yoonda's feelings, but for a totally different reason. Yebblegoot's old wife was jealous, for she knew that her husband would transfer his affections to the girl as soon as they were married.

When a young man from a distant but related clan paid them a visit,

---

* It might be expected that the seed-pod would be contained in the mother and so personified; but in Aboriginal myth the male element is frequently regarded as the important procreative power.

she encouraged him to take an interest in the younger woman. Boojin needed no encouragement. Yoonda was the most beautiful girl he had ever seen. He fell in love with her and determined to take her to wife, no matter what the consequence might be. He was well aware of the danger into which he might lead her, and himself, for vengeance was swift and severe upon young people who broke the tribal laws.

If Yoonda had been unresponsive, it would have been a different matter; but it was soon obvious, not only to Boojin but also the old wife, that the girl responded eagerly to his advances. But the time of marriage was at hand, for Yoonda had gone through all the initiation tests and was ready for domestic work and child-bearing. The opportunity she had been waiting for came on a day when Yebblegoot happened to leave his miamia earlier than usual. Yebblegoot's intention that day was to bring a heavy backload of flesh for the parents of the prospective bride, and then to press for early consummation of the marriage.

The old wife watched until Yebblegoot disappeared on his quest, and called Yoonda and Boojin to her.

'I know you love each other,' she said, and chuckled at the guilty look that crossed the faces of the young people.

'There's no use denying it,' she said. 'What are you going to do about it? Are you prepared to marry my husband, Yoonda? Are you ready to let her go without a struggle, Boojin?'

They looked at each other face to face and read determination in each other's eyes.

'No,' shouted Boojin. 'I shall never let her go. I know she is forbidden to me, but I shall fight for her.'

'You can't do that,' the older woman said. 'The elders would never let you. The law is made to be obeyed. There's another way. My husband is away hunting and I know he will not come back until the light fails. If you go now, you can be far away by nightfall. Conceal your tracks as best you can and he'll never catch up with you.'

Boojin looked again at Yoonda and knew it was the only way. After retrieving his weapons, while she hastily packed a few personal possessions into her dilly-bag, they stole quietly out of the encampment. Where they entered the bush, they smoothed out their footprints by sweeping a small leafy branch across them. Hand in hand they ran swifty towards freedom, apart from their people, but with the prospect of life together.

Boojin used every ruse he knew to conceal their trail, choosing stony ground wherever possible, wading through streams, swinging from branch to branch of trees. He knew there was a concealed valley somewhere in the hills. He had never seen it, but he hoped that somehow he would find it. Yoonda was growing tired. She had to be helped over rough places. While it was easy to cover his own trail, he found it increasingly difficult to conceal her passage through the bush. After many hours she could go no further. He lifted her in his arms and carried her—but now they were travelling slowly, increasing his fear that others might be following.

He was unaware that Yoonda had cut her foot and that a trail of blood showed clearly where they had been as he struggled on, not knowing where he was going.

After observing where the young people had entered the bush, the old wife had followed her husband's trail, running so fast that she caught up with him while the sun was still low above the eastern horizon.

Yebblegoot turned on her angrily when she came in sight, shouting that the presence of a woman would scare away every animal within hunting distance.

'Wait till you hear what I have to say,' she gasped, fighting for breath. 'Bad news for you, husband. Your bride has left you.'

'What do you mean, ''left me''? Don't you know that today I am hunting for meat for the marriage meal?'

'There will be no marriage unless you return at once. She's run away with that young fellow Boojin. I knew he'd make mischief as soon as he came.'

Yebblegoot wasted no further words. Hastening back to the encampment, he soon had a band of warriors eager to punish the daring youngster. In spite of the care that Boojin had taken, it was not difficult for experienced hunters to pick up the trail. In the late afternoon Boojin was travelling slowly while the warriors, hard and fit from many a hunting expedition, drew so close that they could see them some distance ahead.

'Now we've got them,' Yebblegoot shouted. 'Look at that river. They'll never get across. Spread out, men, in case they make a dash downstream.'

Boojin heard the shouting. Straining every muscle, he raced down a long sloping bank and threw Yoonda into the river. Revived by the cold water, she struck out for the opposite bank, closely followed by Boojin. Their courage and determination were rewarded. The river was too wide, too deep, too swift-running for Yebblegoot and his men to venture to cross. They returned disconsolately to their camp ground. For Yoonda and Boojin a new life began that day. They had found their enchanted valley, far from jealous wives and the rage of old men; but in spite of their isolation from the rest of the world, Yoonda left a memorial of her courageous flight for others to see and enjoy.

The drops of blood from her injured foot fell to the ground and blossomed as a flower creeper, the beautiful plant known to white men as the Coral Creeper.

A similar tale comes from Central Australia, where a young woman eloped with a lover to escape marriage with an elderly man. They took refuge with the young man's tribe, and lived there for some years. Eventually the rejected husband organised a retaliatory expedition, intending to take the woman by force and kill her husband, together with all the tribespeople. The expedition was successful, for the woman as well as her husband and all her relatives by marriage were killed.

Some time later the vindictive old man returned to inspect the bones that were scattered over the plain, only to find they were covered with a carpet of scarlet flowers that had sprung from the blood of the young woman. Sturt's Desert Pea is the common name, but to the Aboriginal it is the Flower of Blood.

The Flower Child

The most beautiful of all the flower legends is probably that told to Roland Robinson by an Aboriginal of Lake Cargelligo in south-west New South Wales.*

Long before the white man came, before even the original Australians were here, two sisters walked in fields covered with a carpet of flowers. Where they came from no one could tell, for there were no men in this land. It was the springtime of the world, when every living thing was young.

The sisters strolled among the sweet-scented flowers. At times they went hand in hand, at others they parted in search of edible roots and leaves to satisfy their hunger.

Near the close of a bright sunny day, one of the sisters bent to touch an unusually large flower. Gazing into the petals, she saw the face of a baby. The tiny face was so appealing that she plucked the flower and placed it between two pieces of bark to protect it, leaving it to be washed with the dew of early morning. It was a treasure she felt she must keep to herself. Without saying anything to her sister she visited the flower every day, watching the baby growing and becoming more desirable, every time she looked at it.

Summer passed quickly. When autumn came the nights were colder. The flower had faded. The child was still growing but its little face and hands were blue with cold. She hurried back to the bark hut where she slept with her sister, fetched a piece of soft possum fur, and wrapped the baby in it. The infant smiled at her and her heart turned over. She picked him up and instinctively put him to her breast. The baby lay contentedly in her arms, pulling at her breast and waving his tiny hands.

The girl who had not known a man had become a mother. The time had come to tell her sister of the wonderful thing that had happened amongst the flowers of the field. Together they nurtured the child, played with it

---

* Roland Robinson, *The Man Who Sold His Dreaming* (Currawong Publishing Company).

through infancy, taught it to speak and sing, and bestowed on it the little knowledge they possessed of the ways of birds and animals and how to hunt them for food.

When fully grown the man-child became Mulyan, the Eagle-hawk, and at the end of his life rose into the sky as a bright red star.

Fred Biggs, the Aboriginal who told the story, said in conclusion: 'When I hear the white people preaching, it puts me in mind of this story. That man, Mullairn, was like Jesus. He came into this world without a father. He was formed from a flower. That woman touched that flower. If she had not plucked it, this would not have happened.'

CHAPTER SIX

CROCODILE PEOPLE

Along the northern coast there are two species of crocodile, the fresh-water variety, which is shy and comparatively harmless, and the salt-water kind, which is more difficult to snare but relished as food. This is Pikuwa. In legend the Crocodile Man is a stealer of wives and seducer of young women—a trait that is emphasised in a fragmentary tale from northern Queensland.

Pikuwa and his Wives

Pikuwa was sick. No one would come near him, no one except Otama the Porpoise.

'I'm dying of thirst,' Pikuwa gasped.

'Why don't you drink some of the water you're lying in?' asked the Porpoise. 'If it's good enough for me, it should be all right for you.'

'I want fresh water. Water from the well.'

'Dig your own well,' Porpoise said rudely. 'You've got sharp claws, which is more than I have.'

Pikuwa snapped feebly at Porpoise, who reared up and stabbed him with his spear. Pikuwa, who at heart was a coward, turned and ran to his home close to the sea. His son's wife came to him and said, 'Poor Pikuwa. Let me rub the sore place in your side.'

Pikuwa was pleased when she washed the wound and sang the Crocodile song to him, the song that goes something like this:

I can't go back. I can't go back
On account of the spear in your back.

I'll follow you down to the sea
And you'll live in your auwa with me
There we'll stay
Till close of day
For you can't and I can't go back.

Pikuwa evidently took this as a declaration of love, and invited her to become his wife.

At that moment the mother of the young woman arrived at the auwa.

'Mother,' she cried. 'I'm married to Pikuwa.'

The older woman took no notice. She went up to the Crocodile Man and stroked his wound. The gratified Pikuwa immediately offered to marry her and so became the husband of his son's wife and her mother.

The next to arrive was his sister's daughter, and to her too he offered himself in marriage.

In succession, and on that one day, Pikuwa married his son's wife and her mother, his niece and her mother, his own grand-daughter, his mother, and her mother—and as many of his female relatives as dared approach him.

But he had little time to enjoy their favours. Old-man Porpoise came up and said, 'A bandicoot went down that hole.'

Pikuwa put his hand (or his claw) into the hole and grabbed the bandicoot. Although he tugged with all his strength he was unable to pull it out. It was a miserable death for the Crocodile, with his hand stuck fast in the hole. He refused to let his prey go, and so he died, with his hand in the hole.

The Sad Fate of Pikuwa

From the same northern region comes another tale of Pikuwa, the woman-seducer. Crocodile had conveyed two young women and their mother and father across a river and was wallowing in the mud with little showing except his eyes and nostrils. On reaching the bank the girls climbed an ironwood tree and found honey in a hole in the trunk. Armed with his axe, their father followed them and enlarged the hole, chopping the wood away until it was big enough for him to put his hand inside. Soon the family were enjoying the honey he extracted.

'That's all,' the father said, as they sat on the grass, sharing the meal, while Pikuwa lay watching them with his unblinking eyes. The girls' father wiped his hands on the grass. 'Come on, girls,' he said, and began to walk away, followed by his wife.

'No, we'll stay here and come later,' the girls said. 'Our hands are smaller than yours. There's sure to be some honey left in the hole.'

The girls had a wonderful time in the branches of the tree. When they were unable to get any more honey with their hands, they poked a short stick into the hole, drawing it out and licking it over and over again.

When he was sure that their parents were too far away to hear the girls crying, Pikuwa tunnelled into the banks of the river until he came to the roots of the hollow tree. He climbed up inside the trunk until he was perched precariously above the hole.

'Ow!' he shouted as the stick was poked through the aperture and waggled to and fro in search of the honey. 'Ow! You're hurting me! I'm not a bee. I'm a man.'

The girls drew back.

'Who are you?' they cried. 'Who's that talking in the honey-hole?'

'It's only me, Pikuwa,' was the reply.

The girls looked at each other in dismay. 'The Crocodile Man!' they exclaimed simultaneously. Without their father to protect them, they were frightened of what he might do to them.

They scrambled down the tree and raced along the track where their mother and father had gone. Pikuwa smiled to himself. He was in no hurry. Looking through the hole the girls had used to extract the honey, he watched to see where they were headed.

Sliding down the hollow trunk, he entered the tunnel, crawled back to the river, and let the current take him swiftly downstream until he calculated that he was well past the fleeing girls. He pulled himself up the bank and on to the path, waiting patiently, grinning to himself. Presently he heard running footsteps. As the girls came in sight he reared up, blocking their path.

'I knew you would come,' he said, licking his lips in anticipation.

The girls feared that their last moment had come, and that the wicked Pikuwa would devour them. They fell to their knees and begged him not to kill them.

'Kill you?' he said in surprise. 'Why should you think I'd want to kill you? No, no! You have come to me for your enjoyment—and mine.'

He scratched a deep hole in the ground and persuaded the girls to lie down. There, through the long night, he achieved the ecstasy he had so cunningly planned.

In the morning he sent them into the bush to collect firewood, keeping a wary eye on them lest they tried to escape. They threw the logs down beside the deep hole he had dug. The elder sister asked wearily, 'Do you want us to light a fire?'

'Oh no, not yet,' Pikuwa said with the same wicked glint they had seen in his eye the previous day. 'You must be tired. First come and lie down in the hole with me before you prepare a meal.'

'No,' said the younger sister with equal determination. 'You lie down first. You'll find it more comfortable that way.'

Feeling more than satisfied with this apparent eagerness, Pikuwa scuttled into the hole and lay on his back. As soon as he was settled, the girls piled the logs on top of him. They did not stop until the pit was completely blocked.

As soon as they felt that Pikuwa could not escape, the girls hurried to their parents' wurley.

'Where have you been?' their mother cried.

'We have been deflowered by the Crododile Man,' they sobbed.

'Once?' their mother said.

'No, many times.'

'How did you escape?'

When they told him what they had done their father was uneasy.

'It will only stop him for a little while,' he said. 'Pikuwa is strong. It won't take long to throw the logs aside. Then you'll be in trouble again, my girls. And not only you. Listen to me, and I'll tell you what we'll do. When you hear Pikuwa coming through the bush, call to him and invite him to come to the camp.'

'What will you do, father?'

At that very moment, before their father could reply, they heard a deep voice calling, 'Who is that? Who is talking? Where are you?'

'It's Pikuwa,' the girls whispered in sudden fright. 'What shall we do?'

'Call him, just as I told you,' their father whispered back fiercely, as he caught up his club and spear and sprang behind a tree.

'It's us, Pikuwa dear,' the girls called. 'We're here, waiting for you.'

As he came closer they heard his feet shaking the ground. When he reached the tree behind which their father was standing, a spear flew out, penetrating his ribs. Pikuwa reared up, crying, 'Yakei! Yakei!' He fell on his hands and feet. The girls' father jumped out from behind the tree and struck the Crocodile Man a tremendous blow on the head with his nulla-nulla.

'Yakei! Yakei!' he cried again. Blow after blow rained down on him. Pikuwa begged for mercy, but in vain. He could scarcely drag himself along the ground, his cry 'Yakei! Yakei!' no more than a feeble whisper.

Throwing his club aside, the infuriated father of the victimised girls picked up a heavy ironwood log and finished Pikuwa off with one final blow on the forehead. Drawing his knife, he sawed off the head and bore it back to the camp. When they saw the grisly trophy the women rushed to the place where the body was lying and hacked at it, removing all the portions they needed to make a feast, burying the remaining flesh and bones at the foot of the tree where he had been killed.

'Hit-on-the-head', that place was called. It was where Pikuwa met his end; and ever after Crocodiles have had a lump on their forehead to remind them of the penalty of interfering with young women.

The Pursuit of Numeuk the Hunter

Numeuk was a great hunter. While still a young man living in swampy country, he went in search of geese, accompanied by a friend. Each day they gave the geese they had speared to the old women to cook.

For some reason Numeuk became suspicious of the actions of the women. He confided to his companion his fear that the food they prepared was tainted with magic. The next morning the hunters put out the cooking fires, after having lit a firestick which they took with them.

'If the fires are lit when we return, we shall know that the old ones are preparing an evil magic,' Numeuk said, 'but if the food is uncooked we shall still be able to get the fire going again with the firestick.'

On nearing the camp that evening they were relieved to see no sign of smoke. Nevertheless they approached the site carefully. Peering through the scrub, to their amazement they saw the women holding the geese to their bodies. There was a savoury smell and droplets of fat from the uncooked birds rolled down the women's bellies and dropped on the ground.

This was an evil almost beyond belief. The hunters turned and ran from the scene, their faces distorted in horror. Standing in the shelter of the trees, they concocted a plan to punish the women without hurting themselves. There was great risk to anyone who attempted to harm such evil women, but they were determined to stamp out the women's wickedness.

'There's only one way to do it,' Numeuk told his companion, who was his half-brother. 'We must fight magic with magic. Mine alone is not sufficient. If we combine forces, yours and mine, we shall cool the bodies of those women and cure them of their evil ways.'

They prepared themselves by chanting spells of great power before returning to camp.

'In the morning you are to go to the swamp,' they told the old women. 'We have set fish traps and the fish must be brought back to camp. That is women's work. We shall leave early, so you will not see us until later.'

As soon as it was light the two hunters crept away. When they reached the swamp area they chanted further spells, changing themselves into Crocodiles, and slid into the muddy water. There they lay, with only their nostrils above water.

It seemed a long time before the old women came to the edge of the swamp. They were grumbling at having to wade through the muddy water, saying that it was men's work to take the fish from the traps, and the next moment chuckling to themselves at the way they had tricked the hunters and saved themselves by cooking with the heat of their own bodies.

'We had better get the work over and done with,' one of them said. They waded through the mud and went farther into the swamp until the water was up to their armpits.

'Here is the trap,' said one. Both the women bent down until they were completely submerged, groping for the fish in the dark water. At that moment the Crocodile half-brothers glided forward and caught the head of each woman firmly in their teeth. The longer teeth penetrated their noses, making deep holes in the bridge.

With teeth firmly clamped, the Crocodiles lay still, watching the struggles of the helpless women and witnessing a strange metamorphosis. Their arms grew thinner, spreading out like fans. Their legs dwindled to sticks with flattened webbed feet. Their necks were elongated. Their heads shrank. Their noses grew longer and harder and turned into beaks. Their dark skins were covered in feathers.

When at last they were released they were no longer women, but Geese. And from that time and for ever after, geese have a nasal hole in the upper part of their beaks, as all may see.

From then on Numeuk became the totemic ancestor of Crocodiles. His journeyings took him far from the camp of the Geese Women. At one resting place he was betrothed to a girl named Mardinya, the young daughter of Kunduk and his wife Beminin. As custom dictated, Numeuk then became responsible for providing food for the old couple. As a skilled hunter this caused him little concern, but it put an end to his journeying. Kunduk proved demanding as a prospective father-in-law, never ceasing in his requests for provisions, and demanding the best parts of the animals that Numeuk caught.

After some time Numeuk grew tired of the constant complaints of husband and wife. This became apparent to Kunduk and Beminin. They pacified the restive hunter by promising that he should take Mardinya to wife as soon as she had completed her initiation rites.

'And that will be very soon,' Kunduk said blandly. 'You can see for yourself that she is blossoming into womanhood. She will make a fine wife for you, a good food-gatherer and cook, and be tender and responsive to your advances.'

The puberty rites were over and still Mardinya remained with her parents. 'Tomorrow and again tomorrow' was the excuse that Kunduk always offered. It was not until tribal gossip came to his ears that Kunduk was faced with the loss of his child. The elders accused him openly of incest, the punishment for which was severe.

He hastened to Numeuk and said, 'The time has come! Bring some whistling ducks for Beminin and myself and Mardinya shall be yours this very night.'

'You have lost the little wit you ever had, Kunduk,' Numeuk replied. 'You know as well as I that whistling ducks are out of season. It will be many moons until they appear again.'

Kunduk laughed at him. 'You should trust me,' he said. 'I'm not asking you to chase wild geese. I too have been a hunter. Not as great as you, perhaps, but many things that I have learned are hidden from you. One is the place where the whistling ducks go where hunters such as you can never find them. Wait until tomorrow, Numeuk, and I will show you where to find them.'

Numeuk was still sceptical and suspected treachery of some kind but, he thought, nothing would be lost by waiting another day, with the fresh virginity of Mardinya to be enjoyed at its ending.

His acceptance caught Kunduk by surprise, for the older man had no idea where whistling ducks might be found. In his perplexity he sought the aid of the totemic Goose Women whom Numeuk had punished for their wicked actions. They harboured a grudge against the hunter and were only too willing to do him an injury.

'I can tell you what to do,' one of them said, cackling with laughter like a goose. 'You must take this Crocodile Man who lusts after your daughter to the lake we call Windaramal. Nearby you will find a banyan tree. Pass by it and you will come to a plain where you will find many bones. Remain there and sing this song.'

In her quavering voice that crackled like dry twigs she sang a song that went something like this:

Mumma lies white, bare on the ground.
Mumma's ears are deaf to the sound
Of the whistling ducks in the pool.
The hunter comes, the one who's a fool
Lured by the love of a virgin girl
To see the wings of the ducks unfurl.
Mumma is dead and the ducks are dead
But the hunter will follow wherever he's led.
Mumma, the flesh that is withered and dry
Mumma, the bones that are bleached by the sun,
Mumma that stirs to life for the one
Who thinks that soon the whistling ducks will fly.

Unknown to Kunduk and Beminin there was deep, crafty magic hidden in the words, and dark revenge for the deed that Kunduk had performed in the swamp long years before.

With lighter hearts the old people led Numeuk past the lake and the banyan tree to the plain of whitened bones.

'Now you must listen,' Kunduk said. 'This place is sacred. Only I can show you where the whistling ducks are hiding.'

He crouched down and sang the song the Goose Woman had taught him. Straightening himself, he turned and pointed to a large waterhole that had appeared on the gibber plain. The whistling ducks were congregated round it. Numeuk gazed at it with startled eyes. Never before had he seen so many in one place. Hastily he began to prepare the snares, but Kunduk stopped him.

'I have shown you your prey where you least expected to see it,' he said. 'Let me show you a better way of catching the birds than you have ever dreamed of.'

He presented Numeuk with a long pole.

'This is the way I caught more birds than any other hunter in days long past,' he boasted. 'Hold firmly to one end. Beminin and I will be at the other. We will throw you right into the waterhole. Before the ducks have recovered from their surprise you will be able to kill many of them.'

Numeuk hesitated. The ghost of the words of the magic song, scarcely heard at the time, coursed through his mind: 'The hunter comes, the one who's a fool,' but he failed to identify them.

'Hurry,' Kunduk urged. 'The birds are getting restive.'

Still unsure of Kunduk's intention, but excited at the prospect of killing so many birds at this season, Numeuk grasped the end of the pole. Straining limbs and back muscles, Kunduk and Beminin swung the pole over their heads in the direction of the waterhole. Propelled like a spear from a woomera, Numeuk hurtled through the air and fell through a startled flock of ducks. He braced himself for contact with the water—but no water was there, and the ducks had all vanished. What he had seen a moment before was a mirage, an hallucination kindled by the magic of Kunduk, Beminin and the Goose Woman.

The mumma lay thick on ground that had seemed a pleasant waterhole. Numeuk stood up and walked away from the intolerable stench. Kunduk and Beminin fled, not only to escape the fury of Numeuk, but also the miasmic stink that nearly overpowered them.

There was no need for them to fear the hunter. Numeuk was ashamed of his condition. He was running as fast as his legs would take him to Lake Windaramal to cleanse himself of the evil-smelling mumma. The water closed over his head. He splashed vigorously in the shallows, swam out to deeper water and, returning to shore, scrubbed himself with wet sand. It was all in vain. The malodorous, slimy mumma clung to his skin. Condemned to solitude while it lasted, for animals and insects gave him a wide berth, he set out on his travels once more. At every waterhole he saw he bathed himself again, but without removing the obstinate filth.

But he was not alone. Fearing the wrath of the old men of the tribe, and at the insistence of his wife's brother, Kunduk sent his daughter in pursuit of the man to whom she was betrothed. Day followed day with Mardinya following at a distance. Behind her were Kunduk and Beminin. Until their daughter slept with Numeuk the hunter was obliged, by tribal law, to feed the girl and her parents. This strange quartet went on their way. Numeuk was careful to leave part of the spoils of his hunting each evening for Mardinya to find and share with her parents, who were careful to avoid being seen.

And slowly the awful slime of the mumma wore off until at last Numeuk was able to claim his bride. How great then was his grief to discover that the girl he took to be a virgin had already given herself to another. Casting his mind back to the days when he was living with her tribe, he realised with a further shock that the man who had deflowered her was none other than his own half-brother.

In the days that followed he heard the tearful cries of the girl who should have been his woman. Her parents had returned to their camp. Her husband, now completely recovered from his unfortunate experience, would have nothing to do with her. The young woman was reduced to digging roots and prising witchety grubs from the few trees that remained alive in the arid country through which she and her husband were passing. Her only hope for survival lay with the husband who was yet a husband only in name.

The fires of anger still burned in the breast of Numeuk. Twice he had been cheated, once by Kunduk and Beminin, and once by his bride and half-brother. Never again would he be fooled by smiling faces and false words.

One day the hunter stopped to gather honey from a tree. It was a tricky operation, demanding much care and recitation of many spells. By the time he had cut off the branch that contained the honey, Mardinya had caught up with him and was looking at it expectantly. Numeuk crammed a handful into his mouth and said curtly, 'Come with me.'

He led her to a nearby cliff and placed a sapling against it.

'Climb to the top,' he said. 'You can use the branches as footholds.'

Expecting that he would follow, she climbed the natural ladder and looked pack. Numeuk pulled it away.

'Remain there,' he called.

'Are you not coming?' she called back. Numeuk said nothing. As the daylight faded the girl watched him kindle a fire to roast the meat he had caught during the day. His back was towards her. He remained deaf to her cries.

In the morning he threw a stone up and over the cliff top and smiled as he heard a cry of pain. The next day he did the same, but the girl's cries were weaker. On the third day there was no sound. The stone he had flung disturbed a swarm of flies that had descended on her body.

At last the hunter was satisfied with his revenge. He climbed the cliff and cut off the dead girl's hair, stuffing it into his dilly-bag. Then he returned swiftly to her home.

According to tribal law he was required to give the girl's hair to her parents in token of her death. Numeuk planned a more subtle revenge on the old man and woman who had tricked him. He cut some of the hair into short lengths and mixed them with the honey he had taken from the tree. This he presented to them in a wooden bowl. They received it with delight, believing that their son-in-law had forgiven them.

That night both man and wife suffered severe pains in their bellies. Seeking a cause, they discovered short black hairs in the bottom of the honey bowl. The horror of the truth dawned on them. Mardinya had been killed, and her husband had taken this method of showing his contempt. The outraged parents put their case before the wise men of the tribe, believing that Numeuk would be severely punished for the callous deed.

The elders deliberated long. The clever-men sang incantations and examined the tiny black hairs carefully. To the discomfort of Kunduk and Beminin, they were cross-examined and forced to confess their part in the deceiving of Numeuk.

When the old men were all agreed, they summoned the complainants and told them that Numeuk's dreadful deed was no worse than their deception of him, and that of the girl herself.

'The gods are satisfied,' they were told. 'The weight of Numeuk's evil is now balanced by the weight of your ingratitude and the shame you forced upon such a mighty hunter. We have no more to say, for evil is balanced by evil. It has no further place in our tribe.

But for Numeuk a further ordeal lay before him and a long pursuit that has few equals in the tales that once were told to boys to prepare them for the rituals of initiation. It is a story of hate, fear, endurance, and exhaustion.

Aware that the admiration bestowed on him as a hunter had been diminished by his cruelty in killing his young wife, Numeuk felt the hostility of the tribespeople and set out on a journey that would take him far beyond the tribal lands. While the elders had counselled acceptance of the fact that one wrong had been cancelled by another, there was one who was determined to kill him to atone for the death of Mardinya. He was Mamru, the brother of the dead girl.

As soon as Numeuk had left the camp Mamru followed his trail. He was not as fleet of foot as the famous hunter and soon lost sight of him. Mamru was a young warrior, as yet unskilled in fighting and, under normal circumstances, no match for the mighty Numeuk. But he was confident of success. His mother's brother had given him three stones that would protect him in battle, and he was sure that the burning resentment he felt would strengthen his arm. Being a skilled tracker he was confident that he would not lose the trail and that, no matter how far and fast Numeuk might travel, eventually he would catch up with him.

The pursuit was not as easy as he had anticipated. All his skill was needed to follow the faint trail across the stony reaches of desert. Without the added perception lent by the magic stones his uncle had given him he might well have been at a loss. It was always a relief to come to waterholes where traces of Numeuk's presence were easy to detect; to bush where fallen leaves and flattened scrub, and footprints in soft ground not only showed where the hunter had been, but also how far he was ahead of his pursuer.

It was not until he came to a broad, muddy river, that he met any other tribespeople. Explaining his errand, he sought information on whether Numeuk had crossed the river and if so, how he had managed to evade the many crocodiles he could see.

'Yes, that man passed safely to the other side,' he was told. 'We could hardly believe what we saw. He waded into the water, just like a crocodile, and we saw him no more until he climbed out on the far bank.'

Mamru remembered then that Numeuk was a Crocodile Man and that he must have waded through the mud at the bottom of the river, or swum across barely submerged, without danger from the crocodiles that infested the river. How then could he hope to follow?

The problem was solved by constructing a frail raft of paper-bark stretched over pandanus poles, on which he risked his life—still protected by the magic stones that caused the reptiles to keep well away from the tempting morsel of humanity.

The country on the far side of the river changed completely in character. Instead of sand, rock, and bush, the land was swampy. Mosquitoes plagued him day and night. Huts built on stilts with smoky fires smouldering all night were new to him, but he found the swamp people helpful, and ready to pass on to him whatever information they possessed.

'The hunter passed this way yesterday,' he was informed. 'We warned him there were great dangers ahead if he went on, but he laughed at us. We could see he is a great hunter and a strong man. You are young and lack his strength. It will be best for you to turn back now, before it is too late.'

'What are the dangers you speak of? They can be no worse for me than for my enemy?'

'Numeuk has gone to the country of the Rainbow Snakes,' they said in hushed voices. 'It is a land that no man can enter and preserve his life. The Rainbow Snake Women are the progeny of the Rainbow and Crocodiles. They lure a man to his death with sweet songs and words like honey.'

'How then can Numeuk hope to escape?'

'It may be that because he is a Crocodile Man himself that he will escape.'

'And if not?'

'That he will find out for himself.' They said no more. The only sound that broke the quiet of the night was the whining of myriads of mosquitoes buzzing angrily beyond the smoke haze that enveloped the village of bark huts.

Then an old man spoke up. 'There is a way he can escape their clutches. Somewhere there is a secret path that leads to the womb of Earth Mother. We have never seen this cave, nor dare we go in search of it, for there are perils and magic you can feel in your bones long before you come to it. This Numeuk is a mighty man. It may be that he can discover that secret path.'

'What will he do if he discovers the womb of Earth?' Mamru asked.

'The red earth of the womb is the place of fertility, of the woman-element that can preserve men against women. If he covers his body with his red ochre he will be safe from the Rainbow Snake Women.'

Mamru said no more. Silently he gathered up his spears and set out on the trail left by Numeuk. The Mosquito village people followed him with their eyes, sitting motionless in their huts. Knowing he was determined to follow wherever Numeuk led, they believed they had seen the last of this imprudent young man.

Mamru walked slowly, bending over to make sure he was following the faint trail left by Numeuk. Presently he noticed a displaced twig by the side of the trail. Only an experienced tracker would have seen it, for the trail led onwards without a break. He parted the bushes and saw the merest shadow of a footprint on a softer patch of earth. So this was where Numeuk had turned aside to visit the cave that was known as the womb of the Earth Mother.

He followed the side trail confidently until he came to a tree that towered above the surrounding bush. An old, gnarled man was sitting at the foot of the trunk. He was the guardian of the cave. He looked up in surprise as Mamru drew near.

'You are the second rash one to come this way,' he said in a high-pitched voice. 'Many are the summers and winters that I have sat here alone, yet within three days my rest has been disturbed. What do you want?'

Mamru fell to his knees and laid the spears he was carrying on the grass in front of the old man.

'A peace offering,' he said. 'I have come for the red ochre of Mother Earth to protect me from the Rainbow Snake Women.'

'Always the same!' the old man cackled. 'In all my life as guardian I can count on my fingers all who have come this way, and each of them has made the same request. You may enter the cave and take the red earth, as the man who came before you has done. It may protect you, and it may not. It is well for you that you first offered your gift. The one who came this way but three days since did not display this courtesy, and I opposed him.'

He sighed. 'Unfortunately he was stronger than I. Look!' He showed Mamru a deep wound in his side. 'You would have been less fortunate, for you are but a youth and there is more strength in these old limbs and more craftiness and skill in brain and hands than you will ever attain. But no matter. You have a care for the old, and I can see that you are armed with anger. That may carry you through perils that would overcome others. To say nothing of the three stones I see you are carrying in the bag slung from your neck,' he added craftily.

'Go, my son. You will find the cave of the womb on the far side of this tree. Make sure you cover yourself from head to foot with the red earth, leaving no spot uncovered. Unless you take that precaution, you have no hope of surviving the perils that be ahead.'

He closed his eyes and fell asleep. Mamru circled the tree and entered the dark cave. When his eyes became used to the gloom he saw the red earth glowing with a strange radiance. It was soft to the touch, soothing the weals and scratches that had come with his travels, and warm, even hot, for was this not the very womb of Mother Earth! He smeared his head, body, and limbs with the plastic earth. The guardian of the cave was asleep as he stole past and threaded the narrow path until he came to the trail where Numeuk had turned aside. He felt strangely unprotected without his spears and clutched his nulla-nulla more firmly in his reddened hand.

Presently he heard the siren songs of the Rainbow Snake Women. He came in sight of a tree-girt pool, and longed to bathe in its cool water to wash the hardening red ochre from him. He resisted the impulse. The bodies of the Rainbow Snake Women writhed in the water. They twisted into strange shapes, their heads stretching up to the clouds. He could detect traces of claws and crocodile teeth. More clearly he could see the sinuous coils of their bodies, and knew that without the protection of the red ochre he would have seen only the enticing shape of beautiful women, and have been lured to his death.

He quickened his pace. Surely Numeuk could not be far away. Without warning he stepped out of the shade of the bush and looked down a long, bare valley dotted with huge boulders. At the far end it narrowed to a rock ravine with towering cliffs on either side. The walls sloped inwards, cutting off the sunlight. The path that ran between them seemed black as night, but he could detect something huge and, he felt instinctively, repulsive. It was moving in the darkness.

There was no sign of his quarry in the valley. Mamru realised that he must have passed through the dark, menacing defile, and sat down to think.

'Where Numeuk goes Mamru must follow,' his thoughts ran. 'No man in his right mind would go through that dark tunnel unless he had a purpose.' It was in his mind to turn back. 'But somewhere beyond there must be a fairer land than this. One where it is good enough for Numeuk to make a home. If I turn back now, he who deserves death for what he has done will live long and enjoy the plenty of that land.'

He made up his mind, saying to himself, 'Where Numeuk goes Mamru can follow.'

Holding his narrow wooden shield firmly in his left hand and his nulla-nulla in his right hand, he walked boldly down the valley and into the darkness of the passage between the cliffs. Something hard and unyielding brushed against his arm. In the blackness he saw two eyes gleaming like fire, and heard a hissing sound. The eyes came closer and he realised that something was on the point of attacking him—and that the 'something' was a rock python, larger than he had ever seen before. The head darted towards him in an attempt to stun him as a prelude to being crushed in the coils of the body.

Mamru raised his shield. The jaws of the python closed on it and were pierced by the points at top and bottom. Before it had time to envelope him, Mamru rushed onwards through the tunnel and into a beautiful glade enclosed by high cliffs.

The grass was green and sprinkled with flowers. A stream gurgled over the boulders. Wallabies and other animals browsed or chased each other playfully on the grass or round the rocks at the foot of the cliffs, there was a glint of silver from the fish in the stream, and everywhere the scent of flowers in what seemed like a dream world to the young man who had dared so many dangers in the land through which he had passed.

He wanted nothing more than to lie down and rest in this beautiful scented world. The nulla-nulla dropped from his grasp and he lay at full length on the soft grass, quenching his thirst from the stream that murmured so softly by his head. He closed his eyes and fell into a dreamless sleep.

After many hours he was aware of someone standing by his side. He opened his eyes and saw Numeuk looking down at him.

'You are rested now,' the hunter said. 'I have prepared food. Come and share it with me.'

Still in a daze, Mamru followed him to a cave at the foot of the cliff. A fire was burning on the rocky floor, warming the cave, for a chilly wind had sprung up as the sun disappeared behind the cliff top. Food had been laid out on a shelf in the rock, and brushwood laid in a corner to provide a soft bed.

The two men said little to each other as they ate and then lay down on the mattresses of brushwood. Numeuk seemed strangely subdued. Mamru lay awake, waiting until he heard the hunter breathing steadily in sleep. He rose, picked up his nulla-nulla and stole softly out of the cave. Untying the woven grass bag that hung round his neck, he took out the three magic stones, breathed on them, rubbed them in his hands and, keeping his voice low in order not to disturb the sleeping hunter, chanted the spell his uncle had taught him before he left on his death-dealing mission. He laid the stones at the entrance to the cave and watched them grow.

Soon they filled the cave mouth. Before it was completely sealed he heard Numeuk shouting, begging to be released. A slow smile spread across his face as he watched the stones moulding themselves to the shape of the cave roof, cutting off Numeuk's frantic cries. Without a further care to trouble him now that he had avenged the death of his sister, he lay down to sleep until morning.

Nothing more remains to be told of the death of Numeuk. Avoiding the ravine where the python lurked, Mamru made a rude ladder of laced vines, by means of which he scaled the sheer cliff walls and set off homewards. His journey took many days, for haste was no longer needed. There was time to hunt, to dream by the fire at night, to savour revenge that was sweeter than any sugar-bag, and to rehearse the tale he would tell to the old men when he reached his home camp ground.

The elders sat in a circle nodding their heads, seeming not to listen, though Mamru knew that the words he spoke were retained in their memories, and that some day they might be woven into the stirring tale of how Mamru killed Numeuk the Crocodile Man. For the moment they would neither approve or condemn, but by their silence he knew that all was well.

CHAPTER SEVEN
STAR PEOPLE

Many are the tales told of the scintillating lights that spangle the night sky. The bowl that circles the earth is the last refuge of innumerable fugitives who have found peace and security in the immensity of the heavens.

Sky-raising Magpies

There was a time, before time began, when there was no sun, moon, or stars. The sky itself was clamped firmly to the earth, a belief that was shared by the Maoris of New Zealand. In the Maori pantheon there were seventy gods, sons of Rangi the Sky Father and Papa the Earth Mother, who held each other in tight embrace. It was Tane, the god of nature, who forced them apart to let light into the world and who clothed earth and sky in beauty.

The Aboriginal belief was simpler, though similar in essence. The noisy, garrulous Magpies achieved this stupendous feat. Growing tired of the cramped conditions in which they lived, crawling in their narrow confines with no opportunity of using their wings, they held a conference, from which emerged the suggestion that if they cooperated by thrusting at the roof that pressed so heavily on them, they might be able to raise it well above the earth.

Each bird secured a stick, holding it firmly in break or claw. At a given signal they all pressed their sticks against the firmament. At first there was no movement, but as they strained their feet on the ground and pushed the sticks against the solid mass above them, there was a creaking and groaning like some animal in pain.

'Harder! Stronger! Firmer!' the leader shouted. A crack of light showed on the near horizon. The birds could feel a stirring of the massive bulk. It lifted! Now their feet were leaving the ground. The air between earth and sky was turbulent with the beating of a thousand pairs of wings.

'It moves!' was the cry from a thousand throats as the clinging earth cover moved upwards. The higher it went the easier it became for the birds that pressed on it. For a little while they rested, supporting the mass on the boulders of the higher hills.

Once again there was a concerted effort. No longer did the sky press upon them. It was floating in the air like a gigantic cloud covering earth and sea. The gloom to which the Magpies had been accustomed in their narrow world was lightened, but deep shadows still lay beneath them and above.

The air was colder, the wind keener. Suddenly the sky split asunder from end to end and light such as no bird had ever dreamed of flooded the world. The dark shadows rolled away. Sunshine was there, wind, trees waving in the breeze far below, seas unknown, undreamed of, rolling in blue and white and silver in the golden rays. Untouched now by the sticks that had prised it loose, the sky floated into the immensity of space—a world in itself now that it was separated from earth, a pathway for the goddess of the sun, the god of the moon, and all the starry beings that would some day take refuge in it. Under and around it there drifted a gauzy mantle of clouds.

The Magpies have never forgotten that moment of ecstasy when the sun first shone through the riven sky. Each day that it rises from the journey of night it is greeted by the vociferous chorus of Magpie song, as it was on the day of its first rising.

The fable of the sky-lifting Magpies is by no means universal among the Aboriginals. In another tribe the astounding feat is attributed to a man who, like the Magpies, grew tired of the oppressive confines which he and his people endured. There was so little space in which to move that men and women were as small as ants, creeping through fissures in the rocks. The microscopic hero of the story was a lonely man. Lonely because he dared to question the need for change. Others accepted the conditions in which they lived. This man dreamed of a more spacious world, and because of the dreams he told round the tiny camp fires, he was expelled from his tribe. He wandered far from the campsite, until one day he came to a pool of water far larger than the miserable trickles of water from which he and his people usually drank. Unknown to him, it was a magic pool. Its water gave him strength. He grew in size until head and shoulders pressed against the sky. Bracing his feet, he pitted his strength against it and felt it move. Seizing a stick he thrust it against the sky, forcing it upwards. The stick bent under the strain but by that time the sky was moving. It had needed only a little pressure to send it floating into the infinity above.

As it dwindled into the distance, the man looked round him. Tiny birds and animals were growing in size, as he himself was growing, gazing upwards at the miraculous disappearance of the sky that had pressed so heavily on the earth. A Kangaroo lifted itself up and stood on its hind legs and tail, adopting the posture with which men became so familiar. An Emu ran in circles, its legs and neck growing longer and longer.

The man who had raised the sky lifed his arms and shouted for joy. He threw the bent stick with all the strength of his arms. It described a circle as it flew through the air and returned to his feet. On that momentous day when earth and sky were sundered, the first boomerang made its first flight in the newborn spaciousness of earth.

The unaccustomed freedom was accepted by men, by women, by children, by birds that flew high into the air, by animals, by trees and flowers, by all living creatures except those insects and reptiles who were content to burrow into Mother Earth, who still provided them with sustenance and shelter.

Dinosaurs of the Sky

What is the sky made of? A question that has been asked by the wisest of men as well as children of every race through every age. Is it sufficient to say that it is a 'something', whether a god, as some have maintained, or a land fairer than that of earth, where celestial beings live and sometimes influence the lives of earth-dwellers?

In the trackless heart of the Centre there was once a tribe that came nearer the truth than many wise men have done. 'There is nothing,' they said. 'It is a great hole, a nothingness,' and this is how it happened.

Whether or not the sky was ever pushed into its present position, or whether it was always there, above men's heads, it was once supported on three enormous gum trees. On the earth beneath there were lakes of fresh cool water, fed by rivers lined with trees, and grass grew in the rich soil.

The sky itself was inhabited, not by human beings, but by horrific monsters. From time to time they peered through the tangle of leafy branches on which their land rested and saw the lush fields and forests and the shining lakes far below. It was a fairer prospect than their own sky land. They spent long hours looking at it through the foliage of the supporting gum trees.

It may be that they grew dizzy watching the animals disporting themselves in the waters of the lake, or the swaying of the branches. Whatever the reason, one by one they fell from the sky land until none was left, and only clean-picked bones reminded men of later ages that they had ever fallen from their lofty perch.

Aeons of time passed by. Streams and lakes dried up and the three tall gum trees died. The years and the centuries gnawed at the dead timber, until the trees fell to the ground, leaving holes where the branches had penetrated the sky land. Like a worn out fishing net, the holes grew larger and ran together, until at last the sky became one vast hole, with nothing to remind mankind that once there had been a land inhabited by monsters, held up by three gigantic gum trees. That is why the wise men of the Dieri tribe say that the sky is a great hole. Pura wilpanina they called it: the great Hole.

Under it the land is parched and bare. Few things can live there, for there is no sky land to shade the burning of the heat of the sun in Central Australia. The lakes and rivers are gone, except for salt-encrusted depressions in the sand, but the bones of the monsters of the sky land remain.

The old-time Aboriginals called them Kadimakara, but white-skinned men of today prefer to call them Dinosaurs.

The Seven Sisters

In the sky land or, if it is preferred, the great Hole of the sky, pre-eminent among the stars is the constellation of Orion. It is linked with the fate of seven sisters; and of these sisters many tales are told. Not one is like another except that each sister finds a final resting place in the night sky.*

In one of these tales the seven girls were known as Water Girls. A curse had been inflicted on them. They were condemned to a water existence, confined to a large pool where their only companions were Crocodiles, fish of various kinds, and leeches. They craved the society of human companions, but in vain. There were times when young men attempted to catch them, but these they avoided. Through constant immersion in water their skins became smooth and covered with a slime that enabled them to slip from the grasp of those who attempted to abduct them.

Until one day a hunter saw them and fell in love with one of the girls. Her long hair floated on the surface of the water. The hunter darted forward, seized the long tresses and wound them round his arm. Caught fast by her hair, the Water Girl was unable to escape, and was borne off in triumph.

At first the hunter feared he had made an unfortunate choice, for her nature had changed to such an extent that she was unfitted for life on land. It was not until he held her over a smoky fire that the slime peeled off her body and the curse was removed. From then on she became a perfect wife—and more. Her experience in the pool, in the company of living things, had taught her the language of the animal world. She accompanied her husband on his hunting trips and, by her knowledge of the ways of the wild, ensured that they always returned loaded with game.

---

* An entirely different version of the Meamei is related in *Myths and Legends of Australia.*

The Water Girl's father was also a great hunter and maker of dug-out canoes. The curse that had been placed on his daughters had vanished when one of them was restored to normal life on land. They were all able to return to the camp of their mother and father which, somewhat curiously, was placed high in the branches of a banyan tree.

A few months after they had been restored to their parents, a sad event occurred. To the great concern of all the women, their father had misbehaved himself with one of the girls. The shame was felt by them all, including the elder sister who had married the hunter. She tried to console her mother and sisters, and made a plan to punish the wrong-doer.

One afternoon they saw a small canoe being paddled upstream and realised that their father was returning from a hunting expedition. They watched him tie his canoe to a stake and walk towards the banyan tree, laden with the meat he had brought.

His wife lowered a stout vine, calling to him to tie it to the animals.

'Hurry,' he called. 'I'm hungry.'

'Wait till we've hauled up the meat,' she replied, 'and then we'll let down the vine for you.'

The meat disappeared among the leaves. Shortly afterwards the vine snaked down, the end of it falling at his feet. When he neared the platform built in the branches his wife slashed the vine with a knife and he fell into a billabong and sank beneath the water. His daughters gazed in horror, waiting for him to come to the surface; but there was no movement among the leaves and flowers of the waterlilies until they saw, with renewed horror, a huge Crocodile slithering out of the pond.

A new horror awaited the women. Long after they had given up hope of seeing him again, the dead man rose to the surface and spoke.

'I shall not die!' he shouted. 'Even though I am dead I shall live for ever.'

His words came true, for his spirit lives on, reborn monthly with the waxing of the moon. As it grows, so the body of the dead man is reborn and waxes fat on the spirits of unborn babies, after which he is again torn to pieces by the Crocodile that lies in wait for him.

It happened that in the same tribe there was a woman who, unknown to the men, had stolen the secrets of initiation, and possessed the gift of immortality. She was in league with the reborn hunter, and supplied him with the spirits of the unborn babies when their mothers were careless and failed to obliterate their footprints. He in turn changed those he chose to Water Girls, and so provided himself with physical satisfaction as well as food.

The younger hunter, the husband of the Water Girl he had rescued from the billabong, now enters the story again. He was a good-natured man, seldom troubling himself with the vagaries of his father-in-law and the fate that had overtaken him. Nevertheless the manner of the death of his wife's father must have haunted him, for one night he had a vivid dream.

He dreamt that he was sleeping at the foot of the banyan tree, with his wife resting peacefully at his side, when he heard someone calling her. The voice came from far up in the branches.

'Climb the rope, climb the rope,' the voice kept on repeating. He tried to clasp his wife in his arms to prevent her leaving, but he was afflicted with some form of paralysis, unable to move so much as a finger. Helplessly he watched his wife stand up, clutch the vine that had tumbled from the tree top, and climb up it hand over hand.

Vainly he struggled to speak, longing to call her back, but no sound came. As soon as the girl disappeared among the leaves the strange vice-like grip left him. He leaped high into the air, trying to swarm up the branches in pursuit, not daring to hold the vine lest it break under the double weight. When he was a few metres from the ground he heard a long wailing cry. The severed vine dropped down in snaky curls as his wife plunged headlong into the billabong and sank into the water. The ripples spread. The water flattened itself as though nothing had disturbed it. The leaves of the waterlilies slowly spread over the pond, and all was still.

The young hunter knew then that the wife he had rescued once from the curse of the pool had passed into her father's power, lured to her death by the woman who fostered the father's obscene appetite. He vowed then that he would not rest until he had rescued his wife and put an end to the evil into which she had been forced.

After much searching he came to the home of Nardu, the Sun-dreamer, who provides shelter from the Sun goddess when she returns from her sky journey each night. He reached it as the light was fading.

'What do you want of me?' the Sun-dreamer asked. 'There are few who dare this perilous journey. Your need must be great.'

The hunter told him of the rape of his wife and his desire for revenge on her father and the woman who had aided him.

'Only one woman?' Nardu asked. 'A man, strong and handsome as you, can surely have a choice of wives?'

'It is not my wife alone, though it is she who fills my mind,' the hunter explained. 'She has six sisters who by now have probably been lured back to the dark billabong and deprived of light and happiness. And there are women who fear for their babies because of the wickedness of a man and an old woman.'

'Helping is not the work for which I was destined,' Nardu replied. 'I am the Sun-dreamer. My task is to shelter the Sun goddess, and for that reason you are in grave peril. I must warn you not to enter the cave of darkness. When the goddess comes, and that will be soon, the very rocks will boil with her heat. Do you not see how the plain round you is composed of cinders? Nothing can live in the heat that comes with the goddess. Yet I would help you if I could. If we dry up the billabong where this evil lurks, your wishes maybe fulfilled. That is all I can do for you.'

As he spoke the hunter could feel the goddess burning his skin.

'Hurry!' Nardu said. 'She comes. The goddess is merciful, but mortals cannot withstand her. Go now, lest you suffer the fate that has come to others who have sought her help.'

The young man turned and ran, feeling the fierce shafts of sunlight on his back. He smelled his hair singeing and dared not face the raging torrent of light and heat that poured out of the Sun goddess's cave.

Streams dried up, trees crackled and burst into flame. Far ahead he saw birds and animals fleeing from the devastation that poured from the cave. Darkness had been turned to light, icy cold to unbearable heat. The whole world seemed to be on fire. At last he reached the place where his father-in-law and the seven Water Girls lurked in the billabong.

All he could see was an expanse of dry, cracked mud and a Crocodile struggling to free itself from the mud. Of his father-in-law there was no sign, but far across the smoking plain he could see the seven sisters racing towards a downpour of rain on the edge of the world. They were fleeing for their lives to escape the holocaust the Sun goddess had released. It had served its purpose in burning up the eater of the spirits of babies and his helper, but now the hunter was afraid that the world would be consumed in the flames.

As he ran frantically towards the girls, they disappeared into the curtain of rain. In a few moments he felt its soothing caress on his skin. The Water Girls were still ahead, plunging into the river of the sky where they felt themselves at home. Swimming strongly against the current to the source of the river, they were again lost to sight. Unable to keep up with them the hunter leaped high into the air, up to the very sky where, as a star, he still pursues the seven Water Girls across the night sky.

The Hunter who Threw Stars

In contrast with the somewhat involved story of the hunter who pursued the seven sisters is that of Mangowa, another hunter who saw a young woman paddling a bark canoe across a lake in South Australia. The sight so distracted him from his fishing that he dropped his spear and raced along the bank to intercept her as she stepped ashore.

She tossed her head, refusing to speak to him. Undeterred by her attitude, he followed her to her camp and, in time, so ingratiated himself with the elders that they consented to a marriage between him and the haughty young woman with whom he had fallen in love. As most of the men were old it may be suspected that they had expectations of an improvement in the food supplies, for Mangowa's prowess as a fisherman and hunter was well known.

Unfortunately Pirili did not share the feelings of her elders. It was not unlikely that she had another suitor whom she favoured. If so, Mangowa gave him little chance to court her. He accompanied Pirili wherever she went, except when hunting. From these expeditions he returned bearing gifts—the flesh of wombats and kangaroos, and wild honey, even flowers for her hair, and choice witchety grubs, which are usually gathered by women. Although her eyes gleamed and her mouth watered at the sight of the tempting food, she turned her back when he offered them. And when his back was turned the men and women of her tribe laughed behind their hands, knowing that they would benefit, for the rejected gifts would eventually come to them.

One day, when Mangowa had offered Pirili a particularly tempting morsel, and it had been spurned, his patience came to an end. He picked her up and carried her away, screaming and struggling, heading for the camp fires of his own clan. Some of the younger men pursued him with spears and clubs, but even though burdened with the slight form of the girl, he was fleet of foot. Pirili's cries could still be heard, faint and far away and plaintive in the distance as the young warrior hurried towards the security of the camp fires of his own people.

After travelling for some hours, believing he was nearing the camp ground of his relatives, Mangowa's legs began to ache. His face was scratched and his arms, clamped tightly round the struggling girl, had lost all feeling. He recognised the trees that fringed the familiar clearing, but when he stepped out of the bush, his heart sank, for the camp fires were dead. No sign of life could be seen anywhere. It was then, and only then, that he realised that he had spent months on the far side of the lake in his courtship of Pirili. His love for the beautiful girl vanished in sudden, unreasonable anger. He dumped her roughly on the ground, intending to thrash her with his spear.

It was the moment Pirili had been waiting for. She sprang to her feet and in one tremendous, breathtaking leap her feet left the earth and she soared far into the sky and took refuge in the Milky Way. The women who inhabited that delectable land had been watching her abduction, hoping she would find a way to escape. They took her into their arms, hiding her from the sight of her exasperated lover.

Mangowa had not earned his reputation as a great hunter lightly. The exhaustion of the past few hours was dispelled and he filled his lungs with air, crouched low, and sprang up to the sky.

He could not reach Pirili, who was protected by the women of the Milky Way. In his rage he plucked handfuls of stars as though they were pebbles and hurled them at the women; hoping to drive them back, leaving Pirili at his mercy.

But the women of the sky were stronger than Mangowa. Taking no notice of the flying stars, which dropped down and made holes in the ground that later were filled by the rain and became waterholes, they surrounded the hunter, seized him by the hair and the arms and legs and threw him back to earth.

As for Pirili, there she remains as a shining star in the constellation of Orion.

Wurrunna and the Seven Sisters

The theme of Seven Sisters stars was familiar to the tribespeople in many parts of the continent. In south Australia one of the sisters is Pirili. The legend of Wahn the Crow and the Seven Sisters is probably even better known; in another legend the sisters are Emu Women, who were pursued with amorous intentions by the Dingo Men. They hid amongst the boulders but, as might be expected, the Dingo Men scented them and tried to drag them out. Failing to do so, for the women had wedged themselves tightly into the crevices between the boulders, the Dingo Men lit a fire. The smoke drove the women out, burning their wings, with the result that Emus have lost the power of flight.

With their long legs the Emu Girls were able to escape, and fled to the end of the world where they hid in the sky land and now shine brightly to taunt the Dingo Men who remain far distant, lost in the constellation of Orion.

The culture hero Wurrunna was another who pursued Seven Sisters to their destination in the sky. On his return to the camping ground at the conclusion of a long and unsuccessful day on the plain, he longed for a feed of grass-seed cakes. In spite of repeated requests, no one would give him any. It was not that the supply was exhausted, but that the tribespeople were hoarding them for future use, and would not give them to one who had brought nothing for the evening meal.

Wurrunna was infuriated by their ingratitude. It was not his fault that he had come back empty-handed. Time and time again he had secured game when others had failed. Only this once had he come home without a back-load of meat and they refused to satisfy his hunger! He was too proud to plead with them, too angry to argue. Silently, while his fellow tribesmen looked on impassively, he gathered up his spears and spear-thrower, his nulla-nulla and dilly-bag, and left the camp.

Wurrunna had many adventures as he journeyed to regions that none of his tribespeople had seen. One day he met people who had no eyes but were able to see through their noses. On another occasion he was walking through the bush, and came unexpectedly on a lake surrounded by rushes. The banks were lined with birds, lizards slithered over fallen tree trunks, the air quivered with the croaking of frogs. After drinking deeply of the refreshing water, Wurrunna caught a large lizard, lit a fire, and cooked it in the embers. Presently he lay down, closed his eyes, and was lulled to sleep by the sound of rippling water and the splashes made by the frogs as they jumped off floating leaves and half-submerged logs.

In the morning he woke with dry lips and felt as though sand had crept under his eyelids. At night he had rested on a grassy bank that was cool and soft. Now it felt hot, unyielding, and covered with sharp-pointed stones. He opened his eyes and looked blearily at a gibber desert that stretched to the horizon, dancing crazily in the heated air. Of the lake, the bush, the frogs, or the birds there was not one sign.

The journey across the sandy desert seemed endless. It was bounded by distant mountains that seemed to retreat before him. All day long he toiled over pitiless sands that scorched the soles of his feet, hardened though they were by many a desert walkabout. That night he lay exhausted on the ground, parched with thirst and, as the night wore on, shivering with cold. He would gladly have gathered a few sticks together to light a fire, but there was not a single bush or tree on the plain.

Another day dawned. Wurrunna lay still, hardly daring to move or to open his eyes for fear of what he might see. The ground on which he was lying was no longer stony. Something under his hands was soft and springy. Wind was blowing through the leaves and from far away came the muted roar of a waterfall. It was his ears alone that told him that the world around him had changed for a second time while he slept. There was a freshness in the air. His eyes, when at last he opened them, assured him that the evidence of his ears was true. The grass was a green carpet dappled with flowers. Trees bent over him to shield him from the sun. A river flowed past, wide, still, majestic as it slid beneath its banks and swept over rapids dotted with smooth, shining boulders.

'A magic land! The Dreamland of Baiame!' Wurrunna exclaimed, wondering whether he had left the world of men and been transported in sleep to a spirit world. He detected the smell of meat cooking and saw a thin column of smoke rising behind the trees.

Going forward cautiously, taking care not to be seen, he peered between the shrubs and saw seven of the most beautiful women he had ever set eyes on. No men were there, only the seven beautiful women. He suspected they were engaged on a demanding journey that was the culmination of their initiation into full womanhood. Placing his weapons on the ground, and stepping boldly into the open, Wurrunna held up his hand in greeting.

They looked at him in surprise and with a certain amount of suspicion.

'You look too young for a wirinun,' one of them said, confirming his surmise that this was indeed the final journey on which they set out as girls and returned as women, ready for marriage and motherhood. If so, they were keyed up to a high pitch, ready for any eventuality, and must be approached cautiously.

'Who are you? What do you want?' the same girl demanded.

'You see I come to you without weapons and in peace,' he replied. 'Like you, I am in a strange country, far from the trail of my ancestor. I have seen mysterious sights and at times I have been filled with fear. Now I see you. You will do me no harm. If you share the food you are cooking with me, you will find I can repay you, for I am a skilled hunter.'

The girls laughed.

'Don't you think we can find our own food? How do you think we have existed during the weeks we have spent on this journey? Tomorrow we decorate ourselves with ochre paint. We shall put feathers in our hair and return to our kin as women.'

Wurrunna wisely said nothing. He sat down and allowed the girls to bring him food and water from the river in their coolamons.

'May I sleep here tonight?' he asked when he was full.

'You may sleep by our fire,' they answered, 'but we warn you that one or another of us will be awake all through the night. We trust no man while we are on this journey.'

Wurrunna slept little that night. There was no movement except when one of the girls who had been keeping watch left her station and gently wakened another to take her place. Wurrunna shared the morning meal with them.

'It is time you left,' the eldest girl said. 'If the clever-men ever find out that you have been with us and shared a meal with us we should be in trouble. We are going that way,' she said pointing to the west. 'You must go to the east. You will find good hunting there. We must never meet again.'

They packed their few belongings in their dilly-bags and without a further word or gesture, set out on their way.

Wurrunna sat lost in thought for a while. It was long since he had seen a woman and his ardour was kindled. It would be difficult to carry off one or more of these determined young women, but he was determined to make the attempt. All that day he kept out of sight as he followed the trail. He did not join them when they prepared the evening meal but chewed a piece of dried meat and lay down in the shelter of the bush. The following morning he was up long before the sun rose. As silent as when searching for a sleeping possum, he crept up to the camp and took two of the digging sticks that were leaning against a tree trunk.

An hour or two later there was great consternation when the girls discovered that two of their sticks were missing. Leaving the owners to search for them, the others left the camp site. The two girls whose sticks had been stolen searched vainly amongst the scrub and long grass in ever-widening circles until suddenly they found themselves face to face with Wurrunna.

Before they could recover their wits he grasped them both round the waist and helf them firmy, despite their struggles.

'It's a long time since I have been with women,' he said. 'You had better make up your minds that you are to be my wives. If you do as I tell you we'll be happy together. But if you try to escape you'll be two very unhappy women.'

The girls protested violently, warning their captor that their sisters would soon be looking for them.

Wurrunna laughed. 'By the time they get here we'll be far away.'

'They are more powerful than you think,' one of the girls warned him.

'They'll never find us,' he boasted. 'I'm skilled at concealing my trail, I'll teach you too how to cover your tracks so well that no one can detect them.'

He released them and ordered them to head for the stony foothills, displaying his nulla-nulla prominently to warn them of the futility of attempting to escape.

For the next few days all went as Wurrunna had planned. There was no sign of pursuit. The girls appeared resigned to their fate, and even to show some signs of satisfaction at having been captured by such a handsome man. But they were biding their time, confident that their sisters would come to the rescue.

Late one afternoon Wurrunna called a halt and told them to strip the bark from the tree to cover the saplings he was gathering, in order to make a humpy. As soon as he disappeared into the bush the girls climbed up the trunk and clung tightly to a stout branch. The tree began to grow upwards. When Wurrunna emerged from the bush with an armful of poles, he saw the tree reaching up to the sky, carrying the girls with it.

He was quite helpless. The lowest branches were far from the ground, many times his own height. He called to the young women, demanding that they come down at once, but they were not listening. Far above they heard the voices of their sisters, sweet as the sound of water rippling over stones. The voices came, not from the ground, but from above.

Wurrunna heard them too. The real nature of the seven girls suddenly dawned on him. None of them were initiates. They were sky women who had been visiting the earth to satisfy their curiosity about the ways of men. The two he had captured had probably enjoyed their experience as wives of a mortal. They may even have regretted parting from him, but the call of their sisters was too strong to resist.

As he saw the tiny figures stepping on to the sky land from the topmost branches of the tree, Wurrunna thought he was seeing them for the last time; but he, and all men, still see the Seven Sisters every night when the sky is clear, for they are the Seven Sisters that white men call the constellation of the Pleiades.

The Milky Way

The broad band of misty light that lies across the sky has attracted the attention of many an imaginative storyteller. One of the tales, in which the Milky Way is named Milnguya, centres round an episode in the lives of

Wahn the Crow and Baripari the Native Cat. Wahn is noted for his mischievous propensities, but in this tale he is noted, surprisingly, for his sense of propriety.

Crow and Cat had cooperated in building a fish trap, a low wall of stones that was covered by the sea when the tide was at the full. When it ebbed the fish that had swum into the saltwater lagoon were trapped. The Cat and Crow tribes were therefore ensured of a plentiful supply of fish at all seasons.

The fish that were trapped in this way were usually small, but at one particularly high tide, Balin, the leader of the Barramundi tribe, incautiously allowed himself to be caught by a swiftly-ebbing tide. His exasperation can be imagined; but with the self-confidence of an acknowledged leader, he devised a method of extricating himself and his relatives. He was aware that there was some jealously between the land-based tribes, and considerable resentment that the Wahn and Baripari people reserved the product of their fish trap to themselves. Taking advantage of this, he called to the people of another moiety to capture the smaller fish quickly before Wahn and Baripari appeared, and to release him and his relatives. It was a mistake.

A crowd of excited people rushed into the shallow lagoon and threw all the fish, including Balin and his relatives, on the shores. Pits were dug, fires hastily lit, and by the time Wahn and Baripari and their people appeared, nothing was left but a pile of bones.

The real owners of the fish trap were puzzled at the absence of fish, until they found hot ashes in depressions in the sand and piles of fish bones littered over the beach.

Wahn was more concerned over the fate of Balin than the loss of food.

'Balin was of our totem,' he explained to Baripari. 'You know that I would never dare to eat Barramundi, nor would I want to, for Balin was my friend, the noblest of all his tribe. See, here are his bones, twice the length of any other fish.'

He wept over them.

'What can we do about it, now he is gone?' asked Baripari.

'There's one thing we can do,' Wahn replied. 'We can pay proper respect to his memory. If you can find a hollow-stemmed tree in the bush, bring it here while I gather his bones together.'

Baripari came back dragging a large tree behind him. The two friends lopped off the branches with their stone axes, and placed the bones in the hollow stem, sealing the ends with mud.

'Now what shall we do with it?' Baripari asked.*

Wahn looked up.

'Up there is the river Milnguya,' he said. 'It is quiet and peaceful as it flows across the sky, far away from predators and the wicked ways of men and animals. Let us place the burial post beside its dark waters.'

Holding the hollow tree trunk that contained the bones of Balin by both ends, and assisted by their relatives, they flew up to the river-in-the-sky and laid it on a bank.

'This is a pleasant place!' Baripari exclaimed. 'If it were not for our fish trap I would be glad to stay here for ever.'

Wahn remained silent, thinking deeply.

'We don't need the fish trap any longer,' he said at last. 'Balin has been caught and devoured. Let's leave it to those men below. I am content to remain here with you.'

Baripari was delighted. They lit camp fires and rested beside them.

When we look up at the Milky Way, the storyteller might say, some of the stars are the camp fires of Wahn and Baripari and their relatives; others are the spots of the Native Cat, and for those who can see, the hollow tree trunk that contains the bones of Balin is there, and dark patches that are the outspread wings of Wahn the Crow. And what of the shining mist that straddles the sky? What else can it be than the smoke that reflects the light of the camp fires of Wahn and Baripari?

---

* An entirely different legend tells how a Crow man, disgusted by his quarrelsome relatives, fled to the Milky Way by means of a ladder constructed from the bones of the fish.

Another explanation is that the band of light is the river Milnguya itself, inhabited by a huge Crocodile, its teeth, tail and claws gleaming brightly in the misty light. But for most people, the Milky Way is smoke drifting from many camp fires. In his beautiful book *Wandjina*, Roland Robinson writes of the famous wanderer Nagacork who loved men and animals, birds and fish and reptiles alike.

'Allo, allo, allo, allo, cha nallah, wirrit, burra, burra, cubrimilla, cumbrimilla, Bo bo,' he sang as he went from place to place: 'Oh well, all you people who belong to me, you have changed into men, animals, birds, reptiles, fish, sun, moon and stars. I go now. I go forever. You will see me no more. But all the time I will watch about you.'

And so, when his long pilgrimage was ended, Nagacork took his rest among the stars—and the smoke of his camp fire drifts silently across the night sky to remind us of his friendship with every living creature.

Moon and Morning Star

While the concept of totemic ancestors is paramount in legend and myth, natural objects and phenomena may frequently be discerned as personifications. This is probably true of a northern legend which relates the adventures of two brothers, one of whom represents the Moon, the other the Morning Star. In the original version neither are named specifically, but the influence of the Moon in its various phases becomes obvious when we consider its presence during the dances in which the legend is re-enacted, in its phases and their supposed influence on women, and in the curvature of boomerang and beach. That of the Morning Star is less obvious, but nevertheless an essential ingredient in a simple tale that explains the essential difference between Man and Woman.

One of these brothers we shall therefore call Moon, the other Morning Star.

At the time they journeyed southward, the world was largely unformed.

There were no rivers, few birds, no animals, and little plant life, no sea, and no women. Only blue skies, sun, golden sands. Moon and Morning Star were carefree and light-hearted. They danced as they made their long trek to an unknown destination and, as darkness fell on the world, wrestled together until they sank exhausted to rest.

Food was needed to sustain them on their long trek. They longed for the flesh of fish to supplement the meagre diet of thin roots they found in the dry scrub.

'We need sea before we can find fish,' Moon said when his brother complained. 'Sea and rivers.'

Joyously they created a sea to hurl its waves on a sandy shore, and rivers to refresh withered plants and dusty scrub. Their happiness grew larger, and the chanting song Te-tyampa louder, as they speared fish and cooked them in the ashes of fire. And all the time, whether walking, dancing, swimming, or wrestling they chanted Te-tyampa over and over again.

They carved the land into pleasing shapes, hurling their boomerangs in a vast curve, forming beds for rivers that were yet to run. The clouds gathered on the hills, pouring refreshing rain on a thousand plants that sprang to life when touched by the magic of water. Shining rivulets coursed down the wakening gullies, joined hands and filled the waiting ravines.

Leaving behind them a world that was as fresh and exciting as their own experience in creating it, they came at length to a place to which they gave the name Untyapalanga. Singing Te-tyampa as they wrestled together, Moon encouraged his brother to greater effort. He bounded high in the air, clapped his hands and feet together, and finally sank exhausted at his brother's feet. Moon waited until he was sure Morning Star was asleep. It was the moment he had been waiting for.

Only one thing had irked him during the long journey. He had been conscious of a something missing. Something he craved without knowing what it was. At first he had been content with the companionship of his beloved brother, but as the days passed he felt growing dissatisfaction. It was a missing something so real that it hurt, physically as well as mentally.

A longing, a yearning for the unknown, unrealised, unfulfilled. Yes, unfulfilled. Small river yielded to larger river. Land embraced the advances of the sea. Clouds melted one into another. Even the boomerang that carved the world into shape and the spear that plunged and withdrew and plunged again, transforming the life he had created into death, all these had a purpose and a fulfilment denied to him. Mind, arms, loins, his whole body ached in a longing for the unknown and unattainable—and suddenly, here at Untyapalanga, he knew what it was.

The acts of creation had been shared with his brother, but Moon and Morning Star had acted independently. Each was Creator in his own right. In wrestling they had touched each other's bodies, in singing their voices had blended; but the products of their creation embodied an element that was missing in their own relationship—the ecstatic satisfaction of union, of creation that was the product of two creators. There must be a giving partner and a receiving partner, a strong one and a weaker one whose strength could be greater than that of the giver.

Male and female! That was what was missing! He could see it clearly now. The sky gave rain to the earth which accepted the fertilising element to clothe herself with life. Birds, fish, animals, plants—these he and Morning Star had created, but their creations were greater than their creators, for in their union was the gift of endless, ever-continuing life. Without it they would ultimately crumble to dust. With it grasshopper, worm, seabird, fish, and animal would perpetuate themselves.

And more! Surely there was an ultimate satisfication in this newly discovered act of creation.

He looked down at his brother. His body was illuminated fitfully by the uncertain light of the camp fire. Taking his boomerang, he went over the unconscious form of his brother, using the weapon as a surgical instrument, carving deeply into the flesh, rebuilding the body to a new and, to his eyes, a more pleasing form. As he worked the night passed swiftly. A hush had fallen on the world as though it held its breath to await the creation of the final mystery.

When the sun rose, Moon's work was complete. He threw his boomerang away. No longer was it needed to make life. The brother who had shared his life was ready for a new era of creation. Brother no longer, but woman, wife, co-creator.

So these two, who once had laughed and sung and wrestled together, were joined in a new relationship. There was new meaning as they sang Te-tyampa together, greater joy as they wrestled by sunlight, moonlight, starlight; and utter contentment as they rested in each other's arms at the end of a long day.

Moon lashed their spears together and fashioned them into a yamstick, the symbol of woman's responsibility in life. She used it to dig for roots and insects while with a new spear and a new boomerang he became the hunter of game on land and sea. He the provider, she the help-mate, the one who cooked and carried the dilly-bag and, in her body, and later in the coolamon he made for her, the baby that was born of their union.

So the first woman was made to help the first man, to be the complement of man, as Morning Star in the sky is to Moon.

In recognition of their mating, each month we, who are descended from this first couple, can see in the sickle of the moon the shape of the bomerang with which the first woman was made.

CHAPTER EIGHT
CROW PEOPLE

A parallel to Wahn, the Black Crow, can be found in the folklore of most nations in the world—amusing and ingenious creatures such as Anansi the spider in Africa, the mischievous Polynesian demigod Maui, Hoki the trickster of Scandinavia, and many another.

The following group of legends provides some insight into the spirit of fun and light-heartedness that characterised the Aboriginals in their moments of relaxation. The inhospitable world in which many of them lived was not regarded as hostile, for they were ever under the protection and surrounded by the continually reborn and revitalising presence of their ancestors so long as they remained within the province of their journeys.

The malicious acts of Wahn were as agreeable to those who listened to the tales as those rare occasions when he evinced a more charitable attitude towards his fellows. The selection is a small one from a considerable repertoire of legends in which the Crow appears, with variations in the spelling and pronunciation of his name.

Leaving Home

When Wahn was still a boy, he was already a good mimic, able to imitate the cries of animals and the call of birds. He was popular with everyone, not only with his companions, but also with men and women, who laughed at the fanciful tales he made up for their amusement. As a result of this popularity he became spoilt. The initiation period was a great trial to him, but with considerable ingenuity he managed to avoid some of the more demanding tests. By the time he came to full manhood, he was lazy and conceited, resting in the shade whenever he could, surrounded by a few admiring women who neglected their duties to be with him.

The men of his clan viewed him in a different light. At the meeting of the council they complained that he was making the women lazy too, and decided that he had better leave.

'Very well,' Wahn said when they conveyed their decision. 'If you don't appreciate me I will go, but I warn you that you'll be sorry.'

He gathered his few belongings together, placing some food in his dilly-bag, together with a rope of hair, a firestick and a kangaroo bone. Taking his spears and a throwing stick he had not used for many moons, he left the camp site, to the relief of the men and the regret of many of the women.

After travelling for some time in the territory of his own people, he came across a waterhole beside a few gum trees, not far from the encampment of another clan, and made preparations for a camp of his own. For the first time in years he toiled for days building two rows of miamias, constructed of branches and brush, thatched with grass. Late one afternoon he lit a fire and climbed into one of the gum trees where he was concealed by the foliage. As darkness crept across the plain he watched the hunters returning to their camp site. They looked warily at the new encampment with the many miamias, but apart from keeping a close watch on it, decided not to investigate any further lest the visitors prove to be too numerous to attack.

When it was quite dark a hunter who was returning heavily laden with the body of a kangaroo, and who had been delayed by the weight of his burden, was attracted to the fire in the newly made camp.

Wahn slipped down from his perch and went into the nearest hut, where he began to cry aloud like a baby. Peeping through the crevices in the walls of the miamia, he smiled to himself as he saw the hunter standing and listening. He crept into the next hut, where he imitated the voices of several people, as though they were talking together. From hut to hut he went stealthily in the darkness, imitating the sounds of someone chopping wood, of husband and wife quarrelling, of water boiling in a pot, of running water, of the hissing of steam as water was poured on hot stones, of someone or something thumping on the ground.

When he reached the last miamia in the row he tiptoed into the second row of huts and repeated the performance, speaking with many voices, and with clucking noises and the cries and grunts of animals. In the last hut he sang as a young girl would sing, a plaintive song full of sadness and longing, of laughter and love.

Neilyeri the hunter stood in the doorway, looking for the girl who had sung the song of enchantment. No girl was there, only Wahn, standing looking at him.

'What do you want?' Wahn asked.

'I heard a girl singing.'

Wahn looked thoughtful. 'There's no girl here.'

'But I heard many people, and a girl singing.'

'I tell you there's no one here except me. Come, see for yourself.'

The two men looked in every miamia. Neilyeri scratched his head.

'There's something strange going on. These huts were not here a few days ago. Who are you? Are you really a man, or a spirit? Who made the miamias? Why have I heard sounds of occupation and now they are all empty?'

'So many questions!' Wahn laughed. 'I built them all myself so people would have somewhere to sleep when they visit me. Why don't you stay with me, now you're here? You don't want to go out into the dark do you? We can cook the kangaroo you brought with you and then go to sleep. You'll be quite safe here.'

'No, I'm going back to my own camp,' Neilyeri said hastily. He was convinced there was something eerie about this camp site and that Wahn was being evasive. After all, he had heard all the sounds of a busy community and suddenly the whole camp was silent and deserted. There was some devilment here.

He picked up the body of the kangaroo he had flung to the ground when he had heard the song. Outside the circle of firelight everything was black.

There were no stars, but as his eyes became accustomed to the darkness, he could see the twinkling of the camp fire of his own people in the distance.

A soft voice spoke at his shoulder.

'Don't worry,' Wahn comforted him. He took the body of the kangaroo from his shoulder. 'Come and warm yourself by the fire.'

Neilyeri spread out his hands to warm them. Wahn was behind him. He gave Neilyeri a push that plunged him into the fire. The flames licked round his body, flared up as it caught his hair, and slowly consumed his flesh.

'This is the life for me!' Wahn said as he raked away the ashes and placed the meat Neilyeri had brought on the hot stones, covering it with leaves and earth. When the meat was cooked he ate until he could eat no more.

The kangaroo meat, together with roots and the greens he had gathered, lasted several days.

'Plenty of food without having to work for it,' Wahn thought.

After a week the food was all gone. Wahn lured another hunter into the camp at nightfall, pushed him into the fire, and cooked the food he had brought.

For a time all went well, though he found he had to employ different tactics, travelling some distance and choosing men from other clans, bringing them to his camp under different pretexts.

Then came the day of the corroboree when men and women from the various clans, including his own, gathered together as a tribe.

'Where is Neilyeri?' someone asked.

No one knew where he was, nor the hunters who had disappeared from other clans. Amongst those who were missing was Wahn, who had been driven away by his own people, but little thought was given to him.

A young man suggested that there might be a bunyip on the plain, devouring men who hunted alone.

'Nonsense!' said a grey-haired man covered with tufts of down in preparation for the dance and singalong that was to be held that night. 'Bunyips live in swamps. 'They have more sense than men and women who live on dry plains.'

'Tell us what happened to Neilyeri, then, and all the other men who have disappeared since our last corroboree,' the young man retorted.

'Plenty of things might have happened to them. They might have lost their way and died of thirst.'

'No, no,' came a chorus of voices. 'They were all experienced men. They must have been carried away by an evil spirit.'

Someone began a song in which the words 'What shall we do?' kept coming in as a refrain.

A tall lean figure strode into the circle of men.

'What shall we do about what?' he asked with a smile.

Everyone stopped singing and shouted, 'Baiame! It's Baiame!'

And indeed it was Baiame, the Father Spirit, who had been alive since time began.

'What can Baiame do to help you?' he asked. 'I have come to you in the form of a man because I knew you needed me.'

He listened to their account of the men who had gone away and had never returned.

'Remain here,' he said. 'I am going away. For a little time you will see no stars at night. When they shine again you will know I have gone back to my home in the sky. Then the hunters may go out in the morning knowing they will return safely at nightfall.'

Baiame, the Great Father Spirit, stood alone in the middle of the plain. He saw the solitary camp, larger than any other, with its deserted miamias, nestled under the tall trees. Many tracks led towards it, but there were no footprints to indicate that anyone had ever left it.

'Strange,' thought Baiame. He walked over to the tallest tree, swung himself into the branches, and hid among the leaves.

Presently Wahn came sauntering out of the mallee scrub and stood in the shade of the tree. Baiame watched him eyeing a tiny figure trudging across the plain. It was a hunter who had been so far from home that he knew nothing of what had happened at the corroboree. When he was at a little distance, obviously intending to pass the encampment, Wahn went inside the nearest hut.

Baiame was startled to hear the cry of a baby coming from what he knew was an empty hut; but when he saw Wahn going from one miamia to another and a variety of sounds coming from each, he realised what the young man was doing. But the hunter was too far away to hear the many voices, and after a while was lost to sight.

Baiame dropped lightly from the tree. Catching a wallaby in his hands, he swung it across his shoulder and entered the path between the rows of miamias. The sounds that Wahn was making as he flitted from hut to hut were louder now. Last of all came the song that was sung as though by a woman. Baiame walked up to the fire that Wahn had lit, and said, 'Who is singing?'

'There's no one here except me,' Wahn replied, coming out of the hut.

'There must be. I've heard many people in their miamias, and then a song that is welcome to a lonely hunter, sung by a girl who must be as beautiful as the song she sings.'

'No one is here,' Wahn repeated. 'See for yourself.'

'It doesn't matter,' Baiame replied in a tired voice. 'I have walked far today. I'm a long way from my people. May I sleep beside your fire tonight?'

'Of course you may. Bring your wallaby with you. We'll share a meal together and then you may sleep, warm and safe throughout the night.'

As they came close to the fire, with Wahn walking in front of the Great Spirit, Baiame caught him by the ankle, swung him round like a bullroarer on the end of its cord, and threw him into the fire.

The flames leaped up, bathing Wahn in fire. He grew smaller, dwindled to a heap of white ashes. Baiame blew on them. They swirled round in the flames and disappeared like a puff of dust on a windy day.

Baiame clapped his hands and looked up. A white bird was perched on a bough of the gum tree where he had been hiding. The ashes had come together. They had changed shape and had been transformed into a bird, a white bird that, only a little while ago, had been a man who had cried like a baby and sung like a girl.

No longer was he a man, but a bird, the White Crow, watching a star flashing across a starless sky, the star that was Baiame returning to his eternal home.

Then all the stars in the vast void glowed once more with sudden light.

The Gift of Fire

The White Crow left the deserted camp and went on a long journey, sometimes flying to try out his wings, sometimes walking on his clawed feet.

'This is better!' he said as he flew over the tree tops, and was grateful to the unknown hunter who had transformed him from man to bird.

As he flew he began to feel pangs of hunger. He swooped down to a valley and followed the river that bubbled over the rocks. His bright eyes caught a glimpse of a man moving among the bushes. Wahn settled on a convenient rock close to the bank of the river and watched him curiously. The man had gathered a pile of firewood and was sitting beside it, looking perplexed.

'Why don't you light your fire?' Wahn called.

'What's the use?' the man said when he realised it was a bird that was speaking. 'I have nothing to cook.'

'Not for cooking with,' Wahn said. 'If you had fire you could set the grass alight and the emus would be driven into your arms and you'd have plenty to eat.'

'That's true,' the man said, 'but unfortunately I have nothing to light it with. My firestick burnt out while I was searching for wood.'

Wahn laughed, and turned head over heels on the stone he was perched on.

'I'll tell you how to make a fire,' he said. He flew over to the bank and dragged out a piece of dry timber with a shallow depression in the middle.

'Now see if you can find a stick of hard wood with a pointed end.'

The man broke off a length of dead wood from a branch, using his knife to point the end. Following Wahn's instructions, he placed the sharpened point of the stick on the flat piece of timber and twirled it in the palms of his hands. Soon a wisp of smoke rose into the air. Wahn picked up a bunch of dry grass and piled it on top of the smoking wood. The smoke grew thicker. A dull red glow showed through the grass, then a spark, and another gust of smoke. Wahn caught the grass in his beak, fanned it till it burst into flame, and threw it over his shoulder, where it fell into the long grass close to the trees. It blazed up, and in a few minutes trees and shrubs were alight, the wind fanning the flames, filling the valley with smoke. And with the smoke came fire, leaping from tree to tree.

Wahn plunged into the river and stood there with only the tip of his beak showing, while the man ran for his life with the flames at his back. So fast did he run that he overtook the birds and animals that were trying to escape. When he reached the mouth of the valley on the edge of an open plain, he turned. Fitting a spear to his woomera, he hurled it at an emu that had caught its foot in the undergrowth and was trying desperately to release it. The bird collapsed and died with the spear protruding from its breast.

By the time the man had brought it up the valley the banks of the river were burnt bare and covered with twigs that dropped from the skeleton trees and kept smouldering in the ashes. The pile of firewood was gone, but the stones that had been heaped beside it were red-hot and the air above quivering with heat.

Wahn was standing once more on the boulder on which he had alighted.

'Well, you've got your fire now,' he said laughingly.

He helped the man cover the body of the emu with the hot stones until only its legs protruded, and waited impatiently for the bird to be cooked.

When at last the meat was uncovered, Wahn pecked at it, tearing away lumps of flesh and swallowing them greedily, while the man sank his teeth into the meat and the fat ran down his chin.

Before he lay down to rest, Wahn picked up a burning twig, wrapped it in a sheet of bark stripped from a messmate tree that had escaped the holocaust, and placed it on the boulder in the stream.

It was late afternoon when he woke. He opened one eye, and then sat up with a jerk. A small bird was flying up the valley leaving a trail of smoke behind. Wahn opened the other eye.

'Birds don't leave smoke trails,' he said aloud. He looked at the stone on which he had placed the smouldering twig. The messmate bark had gone. He looked up-river again.

Spluttering from the smoke that still hung in the valley, he flew up the ravine at the head of the valley, buffeted by the hot air, until he caught up with the little bird. He gave it a blow with his wing that sent it rolling over on the ground. The twig dropped out of the bark. Wahn swooped on it, but found that it was cold and dead.

He left the place in disgust and flew back to where he had come from. When he got there he found the man was busily occupied in trying to kindle another fire.

'He seems to be growing shorter,' Wahn thought. 'I wonder what he's doing.' As he came closer he saw that the man was twirling the fire-making stick so energetically that the softer base piece had sunk in the ground, and that the man was following it. His feet and legs had already disappeared. As Wahn stood on the boulder and watched with interest, he sank into the hole until only his head was showing.

Down and down he went, until the river seeped into the hole, filling it with water. It began to boil and give off clouds of steam.

'Well, well,' Wahn said and chuckled to himself. 'That's what comes of playing with fire! I must call this place Tu Mauwa, the place where fire was made.'

A tongue of flame shot out of the hole.

' ''Place of Fire'' is right!' he said as he dropped a few leaves and splinters of wood into the fire and watched them curl up and burst into flame.

He was still laughing as he flew away in search of more mischief.

The Medicine-man

'That's where the stick should go. Another one here. A tuft of grass to fill that hole and keep the wind out. Now to brace the poles.'

Wahn the White Crow was talking to himself as he flew from one tree to another, breaking off the branches and carrying them to the gunyah he was building.

'Why are you building it in a tree?' asked Dinewan the Emu. 'Gunyahs are built on the ground.'

'Not mine,' Wahn replied. 'Ground gunyahs are for men and stupid birds that can't fly.'

'Ho!' said Emu. He was so angry that he nearly choked. 'Ho!' he said again to give himself time to think. 'You'll be sorry when the wind blows. It will be shaken right out of the tree. I wouldn't be surprised if you break your neck.'

'The wind will rock me to sleep in my gunyah, Dinewan. Even an Emu couldn't fall through the floor I've built,' he boasted.

He put the finishing touches and lay down in the gunyah. The branch on which the flimsy structure was built creaked and moved in the breeze. Two of the floorboards rubbed together pinching him where it hurt most.

'Ow!' he screamed and jumped out of the hut.

'Tired of it already?' Dinewan laughed.

White Crow was too busy to reply. In and out of the gunyah he flew with his beak full of moss and grass, covering the floor and packing it into the crevices. When it was completed to his satisfaction he lay on his back with his beak and toes sticking up into the air.

Later in the day he was woken from a deep sleep by a quarrel between Emu and Native Companion. Wahn gathered that Emu had taken the Native Companion chickens for a walk and had lost them in the bush. The shouting went on all the rest of the afternoon and half the night. When at last they had exhausted themselves, as well as losing their voices, and had gone off to their own gunyahs, Wahn came down from the tree. He poked his head into the Brolga home, where the Native Companions were settling down to sleep.

'I've heard what Dinewan did,' he whispered. 'He should be ashamed of himself. Do you know what I would do, if I were you?'

'What?' asked Brolga, the Native Companion, irritably.

'I'd heat up some of the red gum of the ironwood tree, and plaster it over his head.'

Brolga's eyes brightened.

'Help me heat the gum, Mother,' he said.

She blew on the embers of the fire until they glowed brightly and they felt the heat on their faces. The gum was placed on a stone close to the fire until it was soft and burning hot. Brolga scraped it on to a piece of bark. He crept quietly over to Dinewan's gunyah and slapped it on top of his head.

Woken from a deep sleep, Dinewan jumped to this feet, screaming with pain and dancing from one foot to another. When at last the pain subsided, he pulled the cold gum off his head, together with a clawful of feathers.

He was up early in the morning while the world was grey and still, and went upstream, where he dug with his strong feet until he found some red gum. Then he hurried back and heated it over the fire.

'What have you got there?' Brolga asked curiously, hoping that Dinewan did not know who had put the ironwood gum on his head during the night.

'Red gum,' said Emu shortly.

'What are you going to do with it?'

'I'll show you, Brolga.'

He picked it up, and before Native Companion could escape, clapped it on his head.

The dancing of Dinewan in the night was not to be compared with the dancing of Brolga that morning. The hot red gum ran down his beak and dropped on the ground. He sprang as high as Wahn's gunyah, higher than the tree tops, high as the moon. When he came back to earth his feet sank into the ground. They made two holes, so deep that rivers flowed into them and filled them. Brolga jumped out, but again he sank into the ground. Wherever he stood, water flowed into the holes.

All the swamps in Queensland were made on the morning when Brolga danced with the red cap on his head.

Wahn came out of his gunyah and hopped down to the ground.

'Why are you wearing a red cap?' he asked innocently.

'Take it off!' Brolga shouted. He lay on his back and drummed his feet on the ground. All the dancing had gone out of him.

'Leave it to me,' Wahn said. 'I am a famous wirinun, especially good at pulling off red caps.'

He caught the gum in his beak, braced himself, and pulled as hard as he could.

'Oh dear,' he exclaimed, 'there's still some left on your head. It won't lift off. Never mind. If I pulled it any more, the top of your head would come off.'

He fetched water from one of the holes Brolga had made and sprinkled it over his head.

'There you are,' he said. 'It will be better now. Lucky for you I was here.'

'It feels a bit cooler,' Brolga said doubtfully. 'Thank you, Wahn.'

'Don't thank me,' Wahn said. 'I was glad to do it for you. But when anyone says, ''What a fine red cap you're wearing!'', remember to tell them that it was a gift from your medicine-man.'

The Eagle-hawk

After his adventure with Dinewan and Brolga, Wahn felt it might be prudent to make a hasty departure. Strangely, he felt a little homesick. He debated the wisdom of returning, and came to the conclusion that as he was no longer a man, but a bird, there was little chance of his being recognised.

He found many changes at the encampment. Several new clans had taken up residence there. Among them was a man who was universally feared. No one ever dared argue with him, nor deny him anything he asked for. When Mulyan, for that was his name, asked for Wahn's sister in marriage, she was given to him at once.

Mulyan took her into the mountains. Neither of them was seen for many moons. It was hoped that the quarrelsome, over-bearing man would never come back. Their hearts sank when they spied him walking towards the camp.

'Where is the lady Mulyan?' he was asked.

'Mind your own business,' Mulyan said so fiercely that they recoiled and asked no further questions.

Shortly afterwards Wahn returned to his old haunts. By perching in the trees he overheard everything that went on in the encampment. He soon learned that his sister had been taken away by Mulyan, and that no one had seen her since. Wondering what he could do to find her, or if that were not possible, to exact revenge on the man who had abandoned her, he fell asleep. He dreamed that he was beating Mulyan with a club until he begged for mercy.

While he was perched on a branch, dreaming this beautiful dream, Mulyan came along the bush track directly below. He happened to glance up and saw a gleam of white feathers amongst the green leaves.

He chuckled aloud. 'Now I remember a secret my wife once told me about her brother being changed into a White Crow by Baiame. If that's not Wahn I'll eat my woomera.'

He sat down to think what he could do to Wahn before Wahn could do anything to injure him. Presently he rose, feeling pleased with the stratagem he had devised. He hurried to the camp and took a digging stick belonging to one of the women.

'That's my digging stick,' a woman shouted. 'What are you going to do …' Her voice trailed off as she saw who was taking it. 'Oh, it's you, Mulyan. I'm glad you want to borrow it.'

Mulyan grunted. He went along the bush track and, in a soft patch of dirt, dug a deep hole, scattering the soil by the side of the path. He placed a large piece of meat on the bottom of the pit and covered the hole with a framework of heavy timber. Tying a cord to cover, he led it over a branch of the tree and pulled on it until it was drawn out of sight among the leaves. His work completed, he sat down among the bushes and waited, holding the end of the cord in his hand.

As soon as Wahn woke and realised that beating Mulyan with a club was only a beautiful dream, he felt hungry. And no wonder. He could smell meat! The meat that Mulyan had placed in the hole was more than a week old and had a strong smell, which was very pleasing to Wahn.

He flew down and walked along the track, his head turning from side to side, his bright little eyes peering everywhere. He came to the hole and saw the meat lying at the bottom.

'A trap!' he thought. 'A man trap, but not a trap for birds.' It would be the easiest thing in the world to flutter down without touching anything and fly away with such a lovely prize.

His decision made, he swooped down, caught the meat in his beak, and with strong strokes of his wings, bore it aloft to ground level. It was a large piece of meat, and heavy. He needed all his strength to lift it. No sooner did he appear than Mulyan released the cord. The lid thudded down, shaking the ground and imprisoning Wahn in the dark hole. Twigs and bark showered down on him as he crouched at the bottom.

'Let me out!' he cried. 'I'm not an animal. I'm Wahn the Crow.'

He heard laughter and a deep voice saying, 'You'll never escape, Wahn.'

'Who is it? Who's speaking?'

'It's Mulyan, the man who married your sister.'

He jerked the cover aside and before Wahn had time to protest, hit him on the head with a stick, leaving him unconscious, but still holding firmly to the meat. He shovelled earth into the hole until the Crow was completely covered and stamped on it till it was firm.

With a self-satisfied smile on his face, Mulyan went off to his gunyah, thinking he had forestalled revenge and equally sure that it was the last he would ever see of his wife's brother.

In the middle of the night he woke with a start. Lightning lit up the gunyah, then came a peal of thunder, and in the middle of it he heard a voice that sounded strangely like Wahn's.

'It can't be!' he exclaimed. 'He's lying dead under the earth.'

But it was Wahn, and a very lively Wahn. While the dirt was falling into the pit, he had struggled to his feet and had tunnelled through the wall of the excavation. He pecked with his beak and scratched with his claws, making the tunnel and then a shaft that led to the fresh air.

By the time he reached the surface he was exhausted. He lay down to sleep. When he woke the stars were shining. He flew over to Mulyan's gunyah and perched on the roof, chanting a song to wind and rain. Clouds rolled across the sky, the rain came down in torrents. The black night was lit by a flash of lightning, and then came the peal of thunder. Wahn's voice grew louder. At that moment Mulyan woke and heard a song, harsher than the thunder, that made his flesh creep.

Sitting on the gunyah roof
Singing in the pelting rain,
Here I pray the gods to send
Thunder, hail, and rain.

'Mulyan will die,' they say,
'He will perish in the fire,
Wahn will be victorious
And achieve his heart's desire.'

Listen to the voice of doom
As the gods draw closer still.
Mulyan, your time has come;
Now the gods will rend and kill.

Say farewell to all your friends,
Look your last on camp and plain.
I the Crow will take your life,
And your call for help is vain.

Gods of rain will flood your camp,
Gods of thunder crash and roll,
Gods of lightning flash and blind,
They have come to rob you of your soul.

Mulyan lay shivering under his kangaroo skin rug. Wahn flew to the doorway and shouted:

Gods of lightning flash and blind
They have come to take your mind.

A flash of lightning leapt from the sky, striking the gunyah and setting it on fire. Wahn bounced up and down clapping his wings with delight.

After a while there was a movement in the ashes, which were all that remained of the gunyah. They whirled and swirled as though blown about by Willy Wilberoo the Whirlwind. Out of them flew a large bird, which disappeared into the dark sky.

Wahn was thoughtful as he walked away. Mulyan the man had become Mulyan the Eagle-hawk. Wahn was not sure which would be worse. And there was something else to think about too. He had not been hurt by the lightning flash but it had come so close that it had scorched his feathers. Others noticed it and began to call him Smoky-White Crow.

The Pelican Babies

Wahn was not particularly enamoured of the epithet Smoky-White, and decided it was time he left his own people to see what the rest of the world was like.

It was getting dark. He had found nothing to eat all day and was tired and hungry. He had almost made up his mind to spend the night in the tree tops when he saw a light flickering in the distance. It was the camp fire of the Pelicans who were eating their evening meal.

'Hullo,' he cried, swooping on a morsel of fish that was sizzling on the fire. 'Thanks for saving it for me, cousins.'

'Who are you calling cousins?' old-man Pelican asked, trying to snatch the fish from Wahn's claws. He was too late. Wahn caught it deftly in his beak and swallowed it in one gulp.

'I'm your cousin from over the mountains,' he said.

'If you're a Booran, you don't look much like one. Why haven't you got a food pouch under your beak?'

Two fat tears rolled out of Wahn's eyes, hung on the tip of his beak, and splashed on the ground.

'I have no need for one,' he said sadly. 'All I have is my little dilly-bag, because there is hardly any food where I come from.'

Mother Booran felt sorry for him and pushed over a sheet of bark containing several pieces of fish.

'Thank you,' Wahn said with a catch in his voice. 'There's more food here than I've seen since last summer.'

'What's your name?' asked old-man Pelican.

'I'm Wahn the Pelican, cousin.'

'Welcome, Wahn,' all the Pelicans cried, fussing round him, asking questions about his other relations, and finally ushering him into a corner of the hut where he could sleep.

In the middle of the night old-man Pelican nudged his wife until she woke.

'I don't believe that fellow is a Pelican at all,' he whispered. 'I've been thinking about it half the night. All Pelicans have food pouches.'

'How can we find out?'

'Let's take his dilly-bag and see what's in it.'

He picked it up and carried it outside. When he turned it upside down a few trifles fell out—a white kangaroo bone, a rope of twisted hair, a firestick, tufts of fur, and a few feathers.

'See, he's been eating kangaroo meat and birds. No fish. I tell you, he's not a Pelican.'

'What shall we do?' his wife asked.

'I don't know, but we must be careful, I'll repeat a sleep-making spell while we go fishing in the billabong in the morning. We'll hide all the babies. When he wakes up and finds we've gone perhaps he'll go away too.'

It was late when Wahn woke up, rubbing his eyes with his wing-tips.

'Coo-ee,' he called, seeing the hut was empty. 'Is there any food for Wahn the Pelican?'

There was no reply.

'Pelicans!' he called, 'Where are you?'

He put his head on one side to listen, but all he could hear was the murmur of insects, the rustling of leaves, and an unusual squeaking sound.

He hunted for food in vain. There was not a scrap anywhere in the camp. Presently he noticed tracks the Pelicans had made in the grass. He followed them until he came to the billabong. The Pelicans were on the farther side, standing in the water darting their beaks in and out and filling their pouches with fish. Wahn went back to the camp and found his dilly-bag lying in a corner of the hut. He could see at a glance that his bag had been searched.

'Nobody can do this to me. I'll show them!' he said aloud. As he stood racking his brains for something to do to pay the Pelicans back, he heard the squeaking noise again. It seemed to come from a gum tree growing by the camp. He circled round it and saw six baby Pelicans sitting on a branch with a net under them in case they fell off. They were so closely guarded by leaves and branches that he was unable to touch them.

He tried to chop the tree down with an axe, but the axe refused to harm the Pelicans. He lit a fire under the tree, hoping to burn it down, but the fire sulked and died.

Then he thought of the Tuckonies, the mischievous little people who live in the bush and have seldom been seen by mortals. They were friends of his. He sang a little song, asking them to make the tree so tall that no one would be able to reach the baby Pelicans.

As insects burrow in the bark
And fire leaps up from hidden spark
I beg you now, dear Tuckonies,
To play for me the tricks I please.

As frogs jump in the billabong
And birds keep singing all day long,
I beg you now, dear Tuckonies,
To pull and stretch the tallest trees,

And lift the mighty trunks on high
Towards the distant sky-blue sky.
I beg you know, dear Tuckonies,
To carry off these chickadees.

Flashes of pink and white appeared between the leaves. The Tuckonies were at work. The topmost branches moved upwards as if feeling their way towards the sky. The middle branches followed, and last of all the branch on which the baby Pelicans were sitting. They squealed even louder and cried for their mothers and fathers.

Wahn encouraged the Tuckonies by shouting and singing. His voice cracked, and has been hoarse ever since. Long afterwards the Pelicans made a joke of it, and said the tree grew so quickly because it wanted to get away from the sound of his voice.

At last the babies were so high that he could scarcely see them. Wahn was rather surprised that the Tuckonies had sent them so far away, for in spite of their mischievous natures, they were kindly little people.

Suddenly he heard a hissing noise. Looking down he saw the Carpet-snakes glaring at him.

'It's the Guridjadus,' he said in surprise. 'Good morning to you, cousins.'

'Never mind about the good morning, cousin Pelican, cousin Carpet-snake, cousin Crow,' a Snake hissed. 'I want to know why you've sent the Pelican babies away up there.'

'It wasn't me,' Wahn said hastily. 'It was the Tuckonies. They were making so much noise that they wanted to get rid of them.'

'Nonsense,' said Guridjadu. 'The Tuckonies knew we were coming. They did it to protect them from us. You don't think they did it out of kindness to you, do you?'

'Why don't you go down to the billabong and complain to the Pelicans?' Wahn asked. 'When they know you've been cheated out of a meal of their babies they may be sorry and give you some fish.'

The Carpet-snakes hissed angrily and glided off into the bushes.

The sun was overhead when the Pelican fishers returned. One of the mothers cried, 'Where is the tree with our babies? It's not there any more.'

'Of course it's there,' old-man Pelican said. He went with her and then looked round in bewilderment. All he could see was the trunk of a tree stretching far up into the sky. The woman had her head thrown back and was staring upwards.

'Yes, it's the tree,' she said. 'All you can see is the trunk, but if you look up you can see that it has most of its head in the clouds. And look! There's the branch with our babies still on it, and the net we made in case they fell out.'

Every beak was turned up pointing like spears to the sky. Wahn couldn't help laughing at the sight.

'You did it!' the woman cried. 'You've taken our babies away from us.'

'Wahn,' said old-man Pelican in a very soft voice, 'I'm going to give you the biggest thrashing you've ever had in your life. When I've finished I'll throw you in the billabong and the fishes can do what they like with you.'

Wahn stopped laughing. 'Let me explain,' he said earnestly. 'It's true that I asked the Tuckonies to make the tree grow tall, but you know they'd never do anything to hurt your babies. It was because old-man Guridjadu and his wife sneaked in to the camp that I persuaded the Tuckonies to save your children by sending them out of reach of the Carpet-snakes.'

He told the lie unblushingly but was embarrassed when one of the mother Pelicans threw her arms round his neck.

'We're sorry we doubted you,' the Pelican leader said. 'But the important thing is to get them down again. The Tuckonies appear to have gone home. Can you sing a tree-shrinking song, Wahn?'

'No! I'm afraid not. I seem to have lost my singing voice.'

'Then will you fly up and bring them down?'

Wahn confessed that that was beyond him too.

'Perhaps you know a tree-climbing specialist?' he added hopefully. Fortunately the Pelicans had plenty of friends. At their call a number of birds gathered to learn what they wanted. There were Parrots and Cockatoos, Curlews and Larks, Emus, Magpies, Kookaburras, Mopokes, Brush Turkeys, Wrens, Kingfishers, Galahs and many others—but not one of them could climb a tree. After them came Goannas, Lizards, and Possums who had much experience of tree-climbing, but they agreed that the feat was beyond their capacity.

Only Tree Creeper was left. He was a tiny bird, noted for his habit of creeping up trees and pecking insects from the bark. He was so small that no one had bothered to ask him. When all the others had declined, he agreed to try. And to the relief of the Pelicans he brought the babies down one by one and restored them to their parents.

While they were being fussed over and fed with titbits of food, Wahn flew silently away. He felt he had outstayed his welcome.

The Singing Frog

Wahn stared in his astonishment at the clearing. He could hardly believe his eyes. Eagle-hawk was sitting beside Wombat. Goanna was walking arm-in-arm with Kangaroo. Platypus and Native Bear had their arms round each other. Frilled Lizard was dancing with Galah. Insects, animals, and birds were talking together. At the foot of a tree Frog and Tortoise were sitting side by side.

'What's happening, Bunyun-Bunyun?' Wahn called to Frog.

'Peculiar. Peculiar,' said Frog, shaking his head. 'There was a big corroboree. Some of the medicine-men said it was wrong for anyone to marry anyone of their own totem.'

Kinkindele the Tortoise joined in, speaking in a deep voice. 'I want to marry a Tortoise girl. It would be ridiculous if I were forced to marry an insect, wouldn't it? And what about you, Bunyun-Bunyun? Would you like to marry a bird and have children with wings?'

'Of course I wouldn't. A nice little Green Frog with bulging eyes is all I want.'

Tortoise and Frog appealed to Wahn.

'Can't you help us?' they asked.

'Come with me,' he said, and led the way. Bunyun-Bunyun hopped along at his heels, followed some way behind by the lumbering Kinkindele. They sat down on the hill-top.

'There are only three of us, but there are many,' Wahn said.

'Too many,' grumbled Tortoise.

'Three wise heads are better than many empty ones,' Wahn retorted. 'Provided one is mine. Listen to me. All we need is to find a way to stop them eating. Their new wives will make their lives a misery. Then the husbands will go back to their proper wives.'

'How do you propose to make them hungry? They have plenty of food.'

'Not me,' Wahn said. 'You two are going to do it, and I'll tell you how.

You are going down to the clearing to dance and sing. They'll be so amused that the men will forget all about hunting and eating.'

'You know I can't dance,' Kinkindele protested, 'and to be forced to hear Frog trying to sing is too horrible to contemplate.'

He pulled his head inside his shell, drew in his feet and lay there, looking like a rounded stone.

'Never mind. He's asleep half the time anyway,' Wahn said to Frog. He whispered his plan. Frog's face split in two with a grin. When Kinkindele woke, the three friends went back to the clearing.

'Listen to me, everyone,' Wahn shouted, flapping his wings. 'Bunyun-Bunyun, Kinkindele and I have something to show you. Gather round in a circle.'

There was a great deal of laughing and pushing as the circle was formed, with the three friends in the middle. Tortoise and Frog retired to the bush. Everyone waited expectantly for their return. There was a gasp of astonishment when slow, waddling old Kinkindele the Tortoise came dancing into the arena on his hind legs. He stood on his toes and twirled gracefully with the sunlight twinkling on his polished shell. He stood on his front legs, then on his head, wagged his little tail, and spun round on the edge of his shell.

'Again! Again!' the spectators shouted.

No one realised that it was not Kinkindele who had been amusing them, but Bunyun-Bunyun, with a coolamon tied to his front, and a polished wooden shield on his back.

Frog kept on dancing. Birds, animals, insects, lizards, and snakes joined in. Clouds of dust rose in the air, the ground shook as they danced and sang. The sun went down, the moon came out, painting them with white light as the dance went on. When the sun rose again they all lay down to sleep.

It was late afternoon before they stirred and began to think about lighting fires for a meal.

'You've nothing left to cook,' Wahn reminded them. 'You've been asleep when you should have been hunting. As there's no food you may as well listen to something you've never heard before. Kinkindele is about to sing for you.'

Tortoise took no notice of the peal of laughter that rose from the crowd. He waddled into the middle of the circle and opened his mouth.

This time it was really Tortoise standing there, but Bunyun-Bunyun was hiding behind a tree, throwing his voice as though Tortoise was singing. He had often practised this in the swamps and billabongs where he lived. At last he had a great audience.

The voice that was thought to be Kinkindele's growled and rumbled, soared and fell like a bird's. It sang of frogs in the pond, stars shining on water, of reeds swaying in a gentle breeze, lightning playing on mountain peaks, birds soaring, insects burrowing, wallabies hopping over vast plains.

Throughout the day and night the song went on. Not one of the animals would have deigned to listen to old Frog singing in the billabong, but to see Tortoise standing there, singing of life as they knew it, made them forget the passing of time.

When the sun rose on the third day, Tortoise could hardly stand and Frog's voice was as croaky as it is today.

'Let's go fishing!' shouted Booran the Pelican.

They all rushed to the water's edge. Wahn went with them, but Kinkindele was so tired that he slumped on the ground and was fast asleep in an instant.

Soon there was an enormous pile of fish on the beach. Wahn fluttered on to a stump and called out, 'You can rest now while I light a fire to cook the fish.'

'Hurry up and get on with it,' they shouted.

'You must have a little patience,' Wahn told them. 'You know that food must never be eaten where it has been caught. Come with me and bring the fish with you.'

Presently he stopped and said, 'This would seem to be a suitable place.'

'No. You must go farther,' said Kangaroo.

Everyone looked at him in astonishment.

'I didn't say that!' Kangaroo said, as surprised as anyone else. He spoke again without moving his lips. 'Come on. What are you waiting for?'

A tumult arose. Some said 'Go,' others said 'No, he said to stay here.' They tried to shout each other down and soon came to blows.

Wahn looked on approvingly. He knew that Bunyun-Bunyun was concealed in the bush. It was he who had thrown his voice, putting contradictory words into Kangaroo's mouth.

Fur and feathers were flying. Blood was flowing. Wounded birds and animals lay on the ground. Wahn wandered off and sat down with Bunyun-Bunyun and Kinkindele, thoroughly enjoying himself as he saw one after another stagger away from the fray to tend his wounds.

After a while, they all crept away silently, ashamed of what had happened, and very tired and sore. Never again would Wombat want to marry Eagle-hawk. The Frilled Lizard would never again dance with Galah. It was the end of what Wahn, Kinkindele, and Bunyun-Bunyun thought to be madness. The fighting was over for all time, but from then on birds and animals, reptiles and insects learned languages of their own and never spoke to those who were not of their own totem.*

Kinkindele and Bunyun-Bunyun turned to speak to Wahn, but he was not there. He had gone to light the fire and cook the fish that were lying on the battle ground.

Tortoise put his head close to Frog's and said, 'I do think he might have said thank you for what you did.'

Frog looked at him.

'Wahn doesn't know how to say thank you,' he said sadly.

---

* The distinction between men and animals must be made clear. It was unthinkable that men and women of the same totem, i.e. with the same totemic ancestor or ancestral spirits, should marry, for that would be incest. While it is true that Kangaroo and Lizard might be totemic brothers, the emphasis in this legend is placed on the bodies of the animals and not on their spirits.

Eagle-hawk Again

'Out!' shouted Mulyan. 'Out of my camp, you rascal.'

He had seen Wahn creeping towards his gunyah, obviously in search of food.

'Don't be too hasty,' Wahn said. 'I've been admiring the effortless way you fly. I wish I could develop your style.'

'You'd have to be an Eagle-hawk first,' Mulyan said disdainfully.

'Well, there's no harm in trying, Mulyan. I'm proud to be your friend. Will you let me join you the next time you go hunting?'

'You're no friend of mine, Wahn, but you can come with me, provided you can keep up with me. I'm off now, so you'd better hurry.'

He flapped his wings so energetically that Wahn rolled over in the dust. He was on the point of saying something but thought better of it. It was as well to keep in with Mulyan until there came an opportunity of showing him who was the better bird.

It was hard work keeping up with Mulyan. Wahn was soon out of breath. Fortunately the Eagle-hawk began to circle.

'What is it?' asked Wahn.

'Can you see what I see?'

'What?'

'There's a nest down there. Obviously a bush rat's. No, I didn't think you could,' Mulyan said. 'There are several young rats in the nest. I'm going down. You can have what's left.'

They flew down with Mulyan still in the lead. By the time Wahn arrived all the rats except one were eaten. Mulyan tossed the smallest one to Wahn saying, 'There, sharpen your beak on that. It's quite enough for a little chap like you.'

Wahn thanked him and flew with it to a tree, where he swallowed it in a single gulp. He rummaged in his dilly-bag and brought out a kangaroo bone, polishing it and sharpening the point. From his perch near the ground he saw an empty nest. He hopped down and buried the bone in the nest with the sharp point uppermost, concealing it in a tangle of grass.

'You and I together, Bone,' he murmured, 'we'll punish Mulyan for being so contemptuous. I'll bring him with me tomorrow. I'll show him the nest. When he uses his weight to crush the grass, I want you to hold up your head.'

'Come quickly,' Wahn said to Mulyan the next day. 'I've found another rat nest.'

'Where?'

'Close to the one you found yesterday. When you left I hunted round and there it was, quite close to the other.'

Mulyan grumbled and seemed reluctant to go, but the thought of another feed was irresistible. When they arrived, Wahn indicated the nest with the sweep of a wing.

'It's empty,' Mulyan said disgustedly. 'If you've brought me on a fool's errand, you'll be too sore to sleep tonight, Wahn.'

'No, truly there are bush rats there. You can't see them on account of the long grass. If you stamp on it as you did yesterday you'll see them. You are heavier and stronger than me.'

Persuaded by the subtle flattery, Mulyan dropped heavily on the nest. The air was rent by the agonised screech, for he had landed feet first on the pointed kangaroo bone. He fell on his side, moaning with pain. Wahn fussed round him.

'What happened?' he asked. 'Oh dear, a spear has gone through your foot. Let me help you.'

He tugged the pointed bone out of Mulyan's foot, slipping it into his dilly-bag.

'There, that's better. Lie down here in this long grass. You'll be quite comfortable. I'll light a fire to keep you warm during the night and by tomorrow you'll feel better.'

As the moon rose high that night, Mulyan woke with a start. He heard two voices. One was obviously Wahn's but he couldn't tell where the other came from. He propped himself on one wing and saw Crow bathed in silvery moonlight. He seemed to be talking to his dilly-bag and at times holding his sides with laughter.

'You did well, Bone,' he was saying. 'Just what I wanted you to do. Did it hurt when he jumped on you?'

Then came the thin, white, splintery voice.

'The sun and moon fell on my head! I bit deep into his claw. He fell over and roared with pain. Let me do it again.'

Sitting up straight Mulyan caught a glimpse of a white splinter of bone sticking out of the bag and realised what Wahn was laughing at. It was not a spear that had pierced his foot but a magic bone that Wahn had taught to wound him. He staggered to his feet, but the pain in his claw was so severe that he collapsed.

Realising he had been discovered, Wahn hastily pushed the bone into his dilly-bag, snatched it up, and flew away, looking for a safe place to hide.

It was daylight when Mulyan discovered the hiding place. Wahn had taken refuge in a small cave.

'Come out!' he shouted. 'I'll flatten you till you look like a sheet of bark.'

'That's no reason for coming out,' Wahn said calmly.

He watched with some apprehension as Mulyan lit a fire by the mouth of the cave. The smoke poured into the cave. Wahn began to cough and splutter, but presently the sounds died away. Mulyan was perplexed. He sat down to take the weight off his injured foot. In the hot sunshine he fell asleep.

The next thing he knew Wahn was calling to him from the cliff top.

'How did you get up there?' asked Eagle-hawk.

'I climbed up here. You didn't know there was a chimney in the cave, did you? You can't get the better of me, can you, Mulyan—ever?'

Mulyan eyed him closely.

'You're browner than you were, Crow,' he said. 'You're a kind of dirty brown now. Brown Crow! Brown Crow!' he shouted derisively, rocking with laughter.

Wahn was disgusted. He flew away and washed himself in a stream, but it was no use. He would always be a Brown Crow.

But Mulyan was never the same after stepping on Wahn's magic bone. He could fly but when he tried to walk he hobbled like a very old bird, because of the magic bone that had gone through his foot.

The Black Swans

After a thousand and one adventures, Wahn had changed. Not physically, except in one respect. With age his dark brown feathers had become darker still, until they were as black as night. He was intrigued by this change. He had noticed that men's hair and the coats and plumage of animals and birds frequently became lighter with age. He had expected that with the passing years there might be some hope of his feathers regaining their pristine purity. Was Baiame punishing him for the tricks he played on others? Had he been too selfish? Come to think of it, he had never tried to help anyone else. The thought came that there had been occasions when others had helped him, and he had never repaid them or even expressed gratitude.

He decided he would try to turn over a new leaf. And the only way to turn over new leaves was to find some in another part of the world.

It was the longest flight he had ever made, past the Mountain where Baiame had his home above the clouds, to the Land of Women, a place where there were no animals of any kind except a few birds.

The Women of that place spent most of their time making weapons—spears, clubs, and boomerangs. Wahn was curious.

'What's the use of making them when there are no animals to hunt?' he asked.

'We make the best hunting weapons in the world,' they told him. 'Sometimes men come here to barter for them. They give us meat to eat and possum and wallaby skins to keep us warm in winter.'

'Yes, I can understand that,' Wahn reflected. 'But if your weapons are so good I would have thought to see many men here. I can see none!'

'No,' they said sadly. 'There are few who come for them. It's so difficult to get here. You were able to fly across the great desert, but there are no waterholes and there are few who have the strength to cross it.'

'That is so,' he said. 'And then there's the lake at the borders of your land. They'd need canoes to get to this side.'

'Oh, we would never let them cross the lake!' the Women said. 'When they reach the shore they leave their gifts and go back a day's march into the desert. As soon as they have gone we paddle across in our canoes, take their gifts, and leave as many weapons as we think they are worth.'

'But aren't you afraid they'll hide in the bush at the edge of the lake and carry you away?'

'Oh, no. There are usually only one or two men who have survived the journey and we are many. And,' they added, 'we have the best weapons.'

'Then I have a surprise for you. As I was flying here I saw many men crossing the desert, heading your way.'

The Women looked alarmed.

'Don't worry,' Wahn tried to assure them. 'I'll fly back and see what they are doing.' With a flick of his tail and steadily flapping wings he flew away.

Arriving at the men's camp site, he hid behind a boulder, his eyes nearly starting out of his head as he saw that every man had an animal of some kind with him in a bag, or fastened to his wrist by a cord. There were wallabies and wombats, rats and dingoes, possums and koalas. A few kangaroos were tied to bushes.

As he watched and listened, the leader rose to his feet and addressed the men. Wahn learned later that his name was Wurrunah.

'When we come to the lake,' he said, 'you must take your animals with you and hide in the bush. Take care not to be seen. I will call on the spirits to turn my brothers into Swans. They will swim across the lake. The Women will see them and chase them in their canoes. Then my Swan brothers will turn back and lead the Women to the bush where we are hiding.'

'They'll never come ashore,' one of the men interrupted.

'That's why we've brought the animals,' Wurrunah said. 'As soon as the Women get close to the bank you will untie the animals and let them run away. The Women are sure to come ashore and chase them.'

'And what will you be doing, Wurrunah, while this is going on?'

'That is the important part, my friend. You will all keep well out of sight. While the Women are hunting the animals I will cross the lake in one of their canoes. I'll take all the weapons I can find, so there will be enough for everyone. I'll bring them back and share them among us all.'

Wahn had heard enough. He crept away to think over what he had heard. He was facing a dilemma. If he told the Women what he had overheard, they would refuse to chase the Swans and the men would have to go away empty-handed. On the other hand he had a fellow feeling for men who had undertaken such an arduous journey, perhaps without result.

In the end, after cogitating for some hours, he decided to do nothing. He flew up to Baiame's Mountain and perched on a rock overlooking the lake. Soon he saw men creeping through the trees and, faintly in the distance, the sound of a bullroarer. That must be Wurrunah, making magic with his tjurunga. He looked in that direction and saw two men changing from brown to white. Their heads grew small, their necks long, their arms turned into wings, and their legs dwindled to sticks. It reminded him of the time, long ago, when Baiame had changed him from Man to Crow.

When the white Swans reached the middle of the lake, the Women caught sight of them. Shouting with excitement, they ran to the water's edge, jumped into their canoes and began to chase the Swans.

As they drew close to the farther shore, he could see kangaroos leaping in the shadows and smaller animals rushing farther into the bush or on to the sandy desert.

Leaving the Swans, the Women leaped ashore and began to overtake some of the animals. Time passed by. A solitary canoe left the bank and was paddled across the lake. Presently Wahn saw Wurrunah returning with the canoe heavily laden with the splendid weapons the Women had made. He landed safely and distributed them amongst his men.

'I've done the right thing by not taking sides,' Wahn reflected. 'Everyone should be happy now. The Women have had the excitement of the chase and a good supply of meat, not only for the present, but for the future as well. If the animals breed there will be good hunting for years to come. And the men are happy to with such a plentiful supply of weapons.'

A sudden thought made him pause. 'I wonder what will happen to the Swans!'

The two birds were swimming slowly and majestically towards the shore. As he looked at them Wahn was knocked off his perch by a rush of wings. His old enemy Mulyan had seen the Swans and was headed for them.

They saw him coming and rose half out of the water, flapping their white wings, calling to their brother for help. Wurrunah rushed to the side of the lake, but there was nothing he could do to save them. Mulyan had reached them. He was pushing them under water and plucking out beakfuls of feathers until they floated in drifts on the quiet water.

Wahn was enraged. Spreading his wings he flew round the mountain, calling to the Crows who lived there, 'Wah, wah, wah.'

His voice carried across the valleys and across plains and forests. Soon hundreds of Crows were flying out of trees and caves in Baiame's Mountain. Wahn opened his eyes in amazement as he saw they were all as black as himself. Like a black cloud they descended on the lake.

Mulyan heard them coming. No one could mistake that distinctive sound—'Wah, wah, wah,' from which Wahn derived his name. He beat the air with his wings, mounting up until he was lost to sight in the blinding sunlight.

The Black Crows flew round the naked, shivering Swans. They plucked some of their own feathers, letting them settle on the Swans until they were completely covered.

'Thank you, brothers,' Wahn said gratefully. 'You have done a good deed today.'

He chuckled aloud as he flew away, imagining how angry Mulyan would be.

And, of course, it will be remembered by all the Crows of Australia that it was due to their thoughtfulness that the Swans of their land are black instead of white because of the Crow's feathers that covered them that day.

The Moon God

After his solitary excursion into philanthropy, Wahn felt the need to revert to his usual self for a little while. A spice of mischief provided a needed contrast to what otherwise would become a colourless existence. It was not that he intended going back to the bad old days. All he craved was a little holiday from a blameless future.

He went off to see Bahloo, the Moon god, who was an old friend. Bahloo was round and white (a very comforting sort of colour to look at for a while). Bahloo lived in a dark cave in the side of a hill. When he saw Wahn coming to him with his tail dragging in the dust and with feathers black as night, a broad smile spread over his face.

'Come in, friend Wahn,' he called. 'You're just in time to help me.'

Wahn subsided heavily on a convenient stone. He didn't really care what Bahloo was doing.

'I'm making girl babies,' Bahloo said proudly.

'That's women's work,' Wahn replied.

Bahloo's smile grew brighter.

'They only think they make babies,' he said. 'If it were not for me there'd be no babies at all. I make them here. When young women get married I give the girl babies to them. As many as they want. Too many, sometimes, I think.'

'Let me make the male babies,' Wahn suggested.

'Oh no. The boy babies are all made by Walla-gudjai-uan and Walla-gurron-buan, the spirits of birth.'

Wahn went off in a huff.

'I only wanted to help,' he said. 'You get on with your baby-making.'

He sauntered outside and sat on a boulder. Presently he grew tired of sitting and thought he would like to fossick for grubs. After a while he went back to the cave.

'Oh Bahloo,' he said, 'forget about the babies for a while. I've found a tree with hundreds of grubs. Come and help me.'

'That sounds good,' said Bahloo. 'I wouldn't mind a feed of grubs. Where is the tree?'

'Come,' said Wahn, and Bahloo followed him.

'Here is my hooked stick,' Wahn said. 'I've already filled my bag with grubs. Now it's your turn. You'll have to climb well up the tree and throw them down to me.'

Bahloo climbed the tree and poked the stick into crevices in the bark, but could not find a single grub.

'Where are they?' he shouted. 'I never know whether to trust you.'

'Higher up,' Wahn replied. 'I've gathered all the ones where you are. You'll have to go much further.'

Bahloo went further up until he found the grubs. As he prised them loose he threw them down to Wahn. Every time a grub came down Wahn opened his beak and swallowed it. When he was quite full he breathed on the trunk of the tree and crooned a little song he had been taught long before by the Tuckonies.

As fire leaps up from hidden spark
And insects burrow in the bark
I call upon the Tuckonies
To play with me the tricks we please.

Quite a while later he called, 'That will do, Bahloo. Where are you now?'

'Oh Wahn,' said a distant voice, 'the tree has grown so tall that I'm right up here in the sky. What has happened to me?'

'You were too greedy,' said Wahn. 'I'm afraid you'll have to remain up there for ever. I don't know how to get you down.'

The Moon god is up there for all time, but he still manufactures babies. At least that is what he believes, and it is true that he may have something to do with it. When he is very busy he lets Wahn help him, but the baby spirits made by Wahn take after him, and are just as mischievous as the Crow.

How Wahn Became a Star

Wahn was growing old. Whenever he thought of the disgrace of being turned into a Black Crow, he tried to mend his ways, but the old mischief kept breaking out.

He was travelling down the Murray River. He saw no sign of any enemies, nor even of the few friends he had. He wondered what had happened to them, whether they might be keeping out of his way. The thought annoyed him. The only bird he came across was Pewingi the Swamp-hawk. He decided to shake off his depression by playing a trick on Pewingi. Perhaps that would cheer him up. Remembering how he had induced Mulyan to jump on his pointed kangaroo bone, he planted echidna quills in the deserted nest of a kangaroo rat and persuaded Pewingi to jump on them.

For several days the poor bird lay helpless, in great pain and unable to walk. Somehow Wahn didn't experience quite the enjoyment he expected from her plight. When she felt better she agreed with Gooloo the Magpie, who had sympathised with her, that it was a miserable thing to do, and that Wahn should be punished.

'All the same,' Pewingi said, 'though he doesn't know it, he's done me a good turn. I was never able to catch a kangaroo rat before, but now the quills have grown into my feet I find I can hold on to them.'

Far down the river Wahn's doubts and depression had grown into an intolerable burden. He had wanted to tell someone about the trick he had played on Pewingi but no bird or animal was there to listen to him.

'Suppose they're hiding because they don't want to hear it,' he thought. 'Oh, suppose no one really likes me! I thought they enjoyed laughing at the tricks I've played. Perhaps I'll never see any of my friends again.'

With slowly flapping wings he flew far away from the river, and came to Mount Gambier. He looked so woebegone, with his feathers ruffled in the wind and the tears running down his beak, that Gwai-neebu the Robin took pity on him.

'Cheer up, Wahn,' he chirped.

'I've nothing to cheer up about,' Wahn said. 'I've done so much harm to others that no one will forgive me.'

'Perhaps it's not as bad as you imagine,' Gwai-neebu replied. 'Your mischief has taught us several useful things. Because of what you've done Men know to light fires when their firesticks burn out. The Swamp-hawk can catch her prey now because of the quills you gave her; and at least you were kind to the Swans.'

As he was speaking a rain squall swept across the mountain. The two birds sheltered in the lee of the rock where they had been standing. As quickly as it came, the storm was over. The sun broke through the clouds and sparkled on the raindrops clinging to the trees.

'It must be a sign that what you have said is true,' Wahn said, spreading his wings with a new sense of freedom. 'My feathers are still black but I feel clean and shining like the rain.'

Then Baiame, the Father Spirit, called 'Come' in a voice like thunder, rolling across the clouds and echoing from the cliffs.

'Come, Wahn, and take your place among the spirits of the sky.'

He picked him up in his hand and set him in the sky, where he became a white star that looks down on the earth and smiles when it sees the tricks men play on each other.

'Well!' Gwai-neebu exclaimed, 'That's the strangest thing I've ever seen. Wahn a star! I wonder whether he's tricked Baiame, just as he's played tricks on everyone else.'

As he flew down to the lowlands he was deafened by the crying of all the Crows in the world. They were laughing and shouting 'Wah, wah, wah,' because the first Wahn had become a star.

They have never stopped talking about it from that day to this.